"What would you say if I told you I loved you?" Serena asked.

Brian felt his heart stop, then begin pounding against his ribs. "I'd say, then why are you planning to seduce Joshua Long?"

"Maybe you'd better think about that, Brian." Her arms went around his waist beneath his jacket and her warm body pressed against his. "Think about it."

He couldn't think about anything except the touch of her, the feeling of her against him. And the sight of those enigmatic gray eyes gleaming up at him. If his body had been stone, he might have resisted her; being human, he just couldn't.

"Rena . . ." His head bent, his lips seeking and finding hers in a touch that was gentle only for an instant. Her response was immediate, total; she became a flame that scorched him until every nerve ending shrieked awareness. He felt the smooth skin of her back beneath his hands, and his mind reeled with a wave of hot, savage desire. Her lips returned his kiss fiercely, as hungry as his own, as desperate.

Then, wildly, she wrenched away from him. There was something pagan about her as she stood, staring up at him. "I won't lose control," she gasped, anger and bewilderment filling her voice. "I won't!" And then she was gone. . .

WHAT ARE *LOVESWEPT* ROMANCES?

They are stories of true romance and touching emotion. We believe those two very important ingredients are constants in our highly sensual and very believable stories in the *LOVESWEPT* line. Our goal is to give you, the reader, stories of consistently high quality that may sometimes make you laugh, sometimes make you cry, but are always fresh and creative and contain many delightful surprises within their pages.

Most romance fans read an enormous number of books. Those they truly love, they keep. Others may be traded with friends and soon forgotten. We hope that each *LOVESWEPT* romance will be a treasure—a "keeper." We will always try to publish

LOVE STORIES YOU'LL NEVER FORGET
BY AUTHORS YOU'LL ALWAYS REMEMBER

The Editors

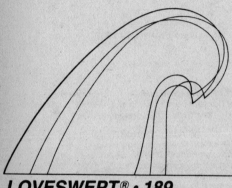

LOVESWEPT® • 189

Kay Hooper
In Serena's Web

 BANTAM BOOKS
TORONTO • NEW YORK • LONDON • SYDNEY • AUCKLAND

IN SERENA'S WEB

A Bantam Book / April 1987

ISBN 0-553-21798-4

Published simultaneously in the United States and Canada

*Bantam Books are published by Bantam Books, Inc. Its trade-
mark, consisting of the words "Bantam Books" and the por-
trayal of a rooster, is Registered in U.S. Patent and Trademark
Office and in other countries. Marca Registrada. Bantam
Books, Inc., 666 Fifth Avenue, New York, New York 10103.*

PRINTED IN THE UNITED STATES OF AMERICA

O   0 9 8 7 6 5 4 3 2 1

for Linda

One

She watched the tall, dark, undeniably handsome man enter the restaurant, watched his graceful progress through the crowded room. She watched the fawning waiters and noted the interested stares of fellow diners. She studied the man's companion for a brief moment. *Blondes*, she thought. *Always blondes. Doesn't his taste vary?*

She looked across the table at her own companion. Another blonde. But the face she studied now was the opposite in every way—except one—from the face belonging to the blonde across the room.

The one similarity was beauty.

Masculine beauty met her thoughtful gaze as she studied her companion. His was an arresting face: lean, classical of feature, tanned, with a determined jaw and humor playing about the curved lips and gleaming in green eyes. A face capable, certainly, of haunting dreams and breaking hearts.

He was a tall man, athletic, with broad shoulders and a lithe way of moving. Thick, silvery blond hair. A man in his mid-thirties who was obviously strong, tough, and determined.

She looked once again at the dark man across the room. Slowly she began to smile.

"You're smiling," her companion observed in a tone of immense foreboding.

She laughed softly and looked across the table at him, her gray eyes as deceptively unthreatening as a silent mountain fog.

"*Why* are you smiling?" he demanded, anxiety mixed with amusement in his deep, pleasant voice.

"I'm not blond, and I don't have blue eyes."

"That's why you're smiling?" He glanced at her wineglass suspiciously, obviously wondering how much was too much.

Her smile widened. "Brian, you're a lovely man. I don't know what I would have done without you these last weeks."

Far from being flattered by these soulful remarks, Brian Ashford began to frown in earnest. "Rena, you're up to something," he said uneasily. "The last time you told me I was a lovely man, I had to bail you out of jail the next day!"

Serena Jameson waved a slender hand in a dismissing gesture. "That was a misunderstanding."

"You bet it was! You misunderstood that cop when he arrested you, so you punched him in the eye!"

Serena gave him another of the gentle, unthreatening smiles he'd learned to mistrust. "He was going to arrest Sam, and I couldn't allow that."

Brian sighed. "I know, I know. Sam was in trouble, so you got yourself into trouble to keep *him* out of trouble—which is the way your mind works! You're *frightening*, d'you know that?"

"Nothing terrible's happened, so—"

"I know nothing terrible's happened . . . this week. Unlike last week. And the week before. Rena, I'm going to apologize to your father if I ever live to see him again. I believed—truly believed—that he was showing needless concern by requesting someone to accompany you from Europe to New York and then on to the West Coast."

"Brian—"

"I never thought," he went on cordially, "that six weeks in the company of a rather lovely twenty-six-year-old woman could hold anything remotely resembling danger. Piece of cake, I thought. Oversee the travel arrangements, keep the lady company, see some of the country I've never seen, and just make sure the genius's daughter doesn't fall down and break a leg during the trip. Easy. Simple. Safe."

"Brian—"

"*However*, no one warned me that you bleed when somebody—anybody—gets cut. No one warned me that your gentle smile and soft voice cloak the heart of an army general bent on victory. No one warned me that the genius's daughter inherited more than her fair share of the parent's brains, and his lack of common sense! And no one warned me that you get into more trouble than a shipful of sailors on liberty!"

Serena looked mildly shocked. "Not *that* kind of trouble, Brian."

Brain gazed imploringly toward the ceiling and

whatever lay beyond. "She's going to get me killed," he murmured.

Reaching across the table to pat his hand comfortingly, Serena said, "Daddy won't blame you, Brian, whatever happens. He's used to me."

Brian employed his free hand to rake through his thick blond hair. "No man in his right mind could ever get used to you," he told her frankly. Then he shook his head as if to clear it. "Look, Rena—your father is very important to my company. If that electronic brain he's developing really works, it'll definitely revolutionize the computer industry. And I really don't mind taking an extended vacation and accompanying you across the country. I could even enjoy it, except for the fact that I'm slightly concerned about two possibilities."

"Which are?" She was gazing thoughtfully across the room, her hand still resting gently on his.

Brian waited until she returned her gaze to him. "One, that you'll get me killed. Two, that I'll murder you."

Serena sat back, her hand sliding smoothly over his as it withdrew. She was still smiling. "Nonsense, Brian." She summoned a waiter with a glance, a trick she had learned from her charismatic father. "You'll feel better after a good night's sleep."

As if he were approaching senility and needed extra sleep, Brian thought irritably. "Rena—" He broke off with a sigh as the waiter approached.

With the gently wistful smile that always won her instant slaves of the male sex, Serena spoke to the waiter. "Would you please have a bottle of your finest champagne sent over to Mr. Long's table and put it on my bill?"

"Certainly, Miss Jameson."

The waiter, Brian observed sourly, was ready to die for her. Then her request sank in, and he began to feel seriously alarmed.

Serena added sweetly, "And when he asks who sent it, just tell him an admirer, would you, please?"

"Of course, Miss Jameson." The waiter, a silly smile on his face, departed.

"What," Brian asked evenly, "was that all about? Who's Long?"

Wide gray eyes gazed at him innocently. "Joshua Long," she murmured. "He's staying here at the hotel, in case you haven't noticed."

Brian glanced across the room and frowned. He waited until the waiter appeared again, following the man's progress as he carried champagne to another table. When he got a good look at the recipient of that expensive bottle, his frown deepened. "I know the name." Then he looked back at her quickly. "Of course I know the name! Rena, he's the closest thing this century's seen to a rake!"

"Exciting, isn't it?"

He stared at her. "I knew you were up to something. Dammit, what're you up to?"

Serena returned the stare, her expression utterly guileless. "Well, Brian, you've convinced me that I need . . . someone to take care of me."

"And so?" Foreboding was heavy in his voice.

"I thought I'd get married," she told him in the casual tone of one deciding which wine might go with dinner.

After a long moment Brian—not trusting his voice—sent an inquiring glance toward Long's table before staring again at Serena.

She nodded. "I should think he'd know how to manage me, wouldn't you?"

Brian ignored the question to ask one of his own. "And is he aware of the treat in store for him?"

If Serena was irritated by his sarcasm, it certainly didn't show on her lovely face. "Not yet. But he will be soon. Very soon."

"Rena, we're going on to Flagstaff tomorrow," he reminded her carefully.

"You can, if you want," she murmured in an absent tone, her eyes once more fixed on the table across the room. "I like Denver. I think I'll stay on here for a few days. Or a week."

"Rena—" Brian began to rise as she did, but he was delayed by the necessity of signing the check. By the time he could catch up to Serena, she was already halfway out of the restaurant. With a choice of two exits, she had chosen the one across the room, which meant she would pass Joshua Long's table. And pass it she did, Brian reflected, unsure of his own emotions as he watched her gliding, graceful movements. She walked, he thought, the way Eve must have walked for Adam.

Long's gaze was drawn away from his blond companion to appreciatively observe that walk, and Brian was near enough to see the arrested expression in the other man's cool blue eyes as Serena sent him a glance over her shoulder.

Catching up to his wayward charge, Brian

grasped her elbow firmly and steered her hastily from the restaurant.

"You spoiled the effect," she told him in mild annoyance as they stood inside the elevator and he released her arm. She rubbed the arm, sending him a reproachful look, and added, "Brute."

"I am not," he said coldly, "going to let you get into trouble again. *Especially* not with Joshua Long. You were unattached when I met you in London, and you'll be unattached when I deliver you to your father in California."

"Deliver me," she murmured. "Like a parcel all tied up with string."

Something about her gentle voice sent Brian's inner alarms—sharpened by the past three weeks —jangling. He backed up rather hastily. "I didn't mean it like that."

"Didn't you?" The deceptively tranquil gray eyes studied him for an unnerving moment. "I believe you did, Brian."

He could think of no response until the elevator let them out on their floor. Then, as he walked beside her down the hall, he said carefully, "Rena, we've gotten to be friends these last weeks, haven't we?"

She sent him a glance. "You've threatened to murder me at least half a dozen times. I suppose that constitutes friendship. Of a sort."

Brian cleared his throat strongly. "The point is that friends watch out for each other. And I wouldn't be much of a friend if I let you . . . get involved with a man like Long. My responsibilities to your father aside, Long would only hurt you."

Serena halted at her door, digging in the spangled evening purse for her key. "I can take care of myself, Brian. I am, as you pointed out earlier, twenty-six, and I've seen something of the world." Locating her key, she unlocked the door and sent him a last, direct look. "I don't need a Galahad."

Brian gritted his teeth. "Long was with someone. Doesn't that mean anything to you?"

Reflectively she said, "I'm not planning to dye my hair blond, so I suppose I'll have to teach him to love brunettes."

"Rena, he'll only hurt you!"

"You forget, Brian,"—she stepped inside the door and smiled very gently at him as she started to close it—"I'm not in his web. He's in mine. Good night."

Serena tossed her bag on the wide bed and stood for a moment in her dimly lighted room gazing at her reflection in the mirror over the dresser. Her thoughtful gray eyes met the reflected ones briefly, then went on to study the rest of herself methodically and critically.

The thick hair piled atop her head was an unusually dark, rich brown, almost black at certain times, but showing coppery highlights in strong light. Her face was delicate, the features finely formed; her large, tranquil gray eyes gave her the unguarded look of a kitten.

She was a tiny woman who appeared amazingly fragile, but her slender figure boasted startling curves that were shown to advantage in the midnight-blue dress she wore; it was low cut and clinging, and though jeans inevitably made her look sixteen, a dress such as this one turned her into a smoky-eyed siren.

Serena sighed softly and shook her head. She wasn't given to longing for what she didn't have, but a few more inches of height and ash-blond hair would have served her purpose better at the moment.

Remembering the blondes Joshua Long had escorted around the hotel during the past three days, Serena sighed again. She glanced at the clock on the nightstand and then sat down on the bed. He'd bribe the waiter to tell him who had sent the champagne, she knew, and would either call or knock on her door. In the meantime, however, she really should talk to her father.

Before Brian did. Serena knew her parent too well to think he'd give Brian permission to spirit her away to California, but she'd always kept him informed of her plans, and this plan was no exception. She placed the call, and shortly heard her father's vague, affectionate voice.

"Hi, honey. Brian hasn't murdered you yet?"

Serena laughed and leaned against the pillows banked up behind her. "Not yet, Daddy. He's threatened to, though."

"Yes, he's called every other day or so," Stuart Jameson said in an absent tone. "He seemed to think I'd be angry that he hadn't kept you out of jail and out of the Mississippi."

"He's being very stuffy," Serena told her father severely.

"Rena, stop playing your tricks on the man!" Her father's tone matched hers now. "I've had twenty-six years to learn how to cope, but he hardly knows you."

"He's learning." She was unrepentant.

"In self-defense, I'm sure!"

She laughed. "He's holding up, Daddy. He may be calling you tonight, by the way."

"What've you done now?"

"Nothing," Serena answered placidly. "Not yet, anyway. It's just that I've decided to get married, and Brian thinks I've chosen the wrong man."

As her father had said, he had been granted some years to become accustomed to her sudden fits and starts. So he didn't deafen her with exclamations of horror or surprise. He merely said politely, "You're getting married?"

"I thought I would."

"And who is it that Brian disapproves of?"

"Joshua Long."

There was a long silence, and then her father murmured, "Joshua Long. I see. He's in Denver? You *are* still in Denver?"

"Yes to both questions."

"And you told Brian you'd decided to marry Joshua Long?"

"Uh-huh."

"He believed you?"

"He doesn't know me very well," Serena explained tranquilly. "Not yet, anyway."

"I see," her father murmured. "I think. Brian disapproved—uh—strongly of these impending nuptials, I take it?"

"Well," she said, faintly dissatisfied, "not strongly enough. But I expect he'll get better at it."

"With a nudge from you?"

"That," she said, "is the plan."

There was silence, and then a soft chuckle. "Rena, when you were a child, I believed you'd gotten few of my brains but all of your mother's sweet temperament. Through the years, I've had to revise that deduction. You got your mother's temper, all right—and my brains—and the cunning of the two pirates and three politicians on the family tree."

"Thank you," she responded gravely. Then her amusement faded. "Daddy? Any more calls?"

Stuart Jameson sobered as well, but his voice was reassuring. "No mention of you since New York, honey. You've lost them, I'd say. Does Brian know—?"

"No, I haven't really found the right opportunity to tell him. I think it's time, though. He's going to be angry when he finds out he's been in the dark during all of this."

"I have a feeling," the elder Jameson said dryly, "you'll know how to handle him."

"Well, I'll certainly try. D'you think it'll be all right for us to stick around here for a while?"

"Yes, but keep your eyes open, honey."

"I always do." Serena smiled to herself. "We'll stay awhile, then, Daddy."

He laughed again. "Then I won't look for you until I see you. Should I start shopping for a wedding present?"

"Just be ready to give me away."

"I hope you know what you're doing," he offered dryly. "Otherwise I'll have to get ready for a funeral. Yours. One of them's bound to kill you."

"Oh, I think I know what I'm doing. See you, Daddy."

" 'Bye, honey."

She had barely cradled the receiver when a knock

sounded on her door. Smiling, she went to answer it, and found a tall, dark, undeniably handsome man leaning against the jamb.

"Thanks for the champagne," he drawled, blue eyes quizzical.

Coat and tie discarded, Brian paced his room restlessly. He was briefly tempted to call the genius who was in charge of the research and development division of Ashford Electronics and give him a piece of his mind. Several reasons kept him from making that call, one of which was Stuart Jameson's probable response. He'd laugh.

Brian had already given up attempting to understand the workings of Jameson's mind. On the one hand, he'd seemed indulgently amused by Serena's plan for a leisurely trip across the country; on the other hand, he had hinted strongly that if someone—unnamed—didn't watch out for his daughter, he wouldn't be able to concentrate on his work. His important work.

He was not the type of genius who threw temper tantrums in order to get what he wanted, or threw his weight around in any other fashion; Brian simply assumed strong paternal feelings and volunteered to escort Serena home from Europe. Jameson accepted the offer instantly, fixing Brian with his vague gray eyes and assuring him that he knew his daughter would be safe in his hands. Completely safe.

The last comment Brian had taken to mean that Jameson wasn't worried his daughter would acquire an electronics magnate as a lover along the way. It hadn't been an implied warning; Stuart Jameson never implied anything. He either said something flat out or said nothing at all. If he said his daughter would be safe in Brian's hands, then that was what he meant. Period.

Finding his charge waiting for him at Heathrow in London, Brian had mentally reminded himself of Stuart's confidence. He'd had no idea of Serena's age then, and had assumed she was leaving school in Europe to come home. When he'd found her in the airport surrounded by the baggage she'd just brought over from Paris, he'd seen instantly that Daddy's little girl was little only in terms of physical size; there was nothing small about her effect on people. Particularly men. Like an oasis of calm in a violent storm, she sat atop a large suitcase and listened with apparent interest while a Frenchman and an Englishman argued in earthy terms about who would have the privilege of carrying her luggage out to the taxi queue. Since both men were dressed in immaculate three-piece suits, Brian gathered they didn't usually do this sort of thing.

Their meeting, Brian knew now, should have warned him of things to come. She had sweetly dismissed her knights-errant upon spotting Brian —she'd seen his picture in the newspapers, she told him blithely—and two skycaps had appeared out of thin air when she glanced around once with a lifted brow.

"Would you have let them fight it out?" Brian had asked her curiously on the way to the hotel they would stay in for several days.

Serena had smiled guilelessly at him. "Of course not, Brian."

She hadn't explained how she would have prevented it, but Brian knew—now—that she would have.

They were three weeks into the trip at this juncture, and Brian had learned that Serena Jameson could do just about anything she wanted—the consequences be damned. He had bailed her out of jail for punching a policeman in the eye, fished her out of the muddy Mississippi River—"But I've always wanted to swim in it, Brian!"—watched her single-handedly start a soup kitchen for street people in one large city and refurbish an orphanage in another city, and carried her bodily from a picket line she'd joined after hearing ten minutes of passionate rhetoric on a street corner.

He was torn between an urge to tie her up and load her instantly on a plane to California, and the fascinated desire to see what she'd do next.

Serena never *tried* to get into trouble, Brian thought with a sigh as he paced. She was soft-spoken, sweet-natured, tenderhearted, polite . . . and somewhere underneath all those gentle layers was the soul of a kamikaze pilot.

She could punch a cop in the eye for threatening to arrest a derelict old man (whom Serena had just met), then tie on an apron and ladle out soup in a kitchen founded—in a single afternoon out of Brian's sight—in an abandoned building while various bewildered businessmen found themselves unloading their personal cars full of contributions of canned goods or their personal wallets of dollars for Serena's cause.

She could dive gleefully over the side of a steamboat on the Mississippi because she wanted to swim, then offer to baby-sit three toddlers so that their mothers could have an hour or so of peace on the boat. She could defeat Brian soundly at poker by dealing with a dexterity that would have had her instantly blackballed in any casino in the world, then drag him to a movie during which she could cry silently over the death of the hero.

She could stand up to the Scrooge-like administrator of a tumbledown orphanage and call him names that had made *Brian* blush, then sit among a group of enthralled children while telling gentle fairy tales.

Three weeks . . .

Brian felt that he hadn't quite dared to breathe during those weeks. It was an emotion somewhere between fascination and horror, leaving him with sleepless nights but a smothered chuckle somewhere deep inside him.

And now—*now*—this enigma of a woman, this gentle, kind, compassionate, sweet, *ruthless* woman had her sights set on the playboy of the Western world. She thought she'd get married. As simple as that.

Restless, Brian paced over to the sliding glass door leading out to his balcony. He went out into the warm night, leaning against the railing and gazing absently over the secluded garden three floors below. Moments later he stiffened unconsciously, his eyes following two people as they walked along one of the winding paths.

The man was tall but virtually unrecognizable in the soft lights concealed in the shrubbery, but

Brian knew the woman; he would have known that midnight-blue evening gown anywhere.

He barely felt the railing cut into his hands as he gripped it, and only half heard the soft curses that escaped without his volition. Damn the woman, he thought, she was really going to do it.

She was going to try to catch a rake.

Two

Brian wasn't quite sure that Serena would show up as usual for their breakfast together. He was early himself, primarily because he'd decided to stay up until after five A.M., watching the sunrise with a jaundiced eye. That was sometime after he'd grown tired of reminding himself that Serena was certainly of age, and it was no business of *his* if she didn't return to her room until after dawn. . . .

If she returned to her room while he was staring moodily at a truly spectacular sunrise, he didn't hear her. And he had his door ajar. Accidentally, of course.

Showering and shaving had given Brian time for reflection, but it hadn't really helped. After three weeks of Serena's nerve-racking company, he could hardly feel anything other than a strong sense of responsibility toward her. She was, he told himself fiercely while narrowly avoiding the amputation of his right earlobe, as incapable of taking care of herself as a week-old kitten.

Never mind, his intellect sneered, that she appeared to have survived quite intact for twenty-six years. That was different. *He* hadn't known her then.

He did now.

By the time Brian was dressed and on his way downstairs, however, he had realized—however reluctantly—that his responsibilities to Serena's father had little to do with his own anxiety. The truth was, he conceded bitterly, he was more than just anxious. And for the simple reason that she had spent the night with another man. Period.

And even though he felt a strong measure of relief when the hostess took him directly to a table in response to his question and he saw Serena waiting for him, Brian quite naturally greeted her with a scowl.

"Good morning, Brian." Serena was cheerful, bright-eyed, and appeared to have slept a solid eight hours.

Brian knew better. With controlled violence, he took his seat, accepted coffee from an attentive waiter, then waved the young man away before he could offer to take their order. Barely waiting for the waiter to absent himself, Brian snarled, "Well, are you proud of yourself?"

"For what?" she asked innocently, sipping her coffee.

Belatedly remembering that they were in a restaurant that was rapidly filling with hotel guests, Brian lowered his voice. But the snarl, though muted, carried considerable force. "For handing

Long another scalp to wear on his belt!" he snapped softly.

"Did I do that?"

"Dammit, Serena—"

"You have a very low opinion of my morals." Her voice was extremely quiet, but something about it drained Brian's anger.

"You didn't sleep with him?" he asked bluntly.

Being Serena, she didn't blush or appear to resent the personal question. "No, I didn't sleep with him. I came back to my room a little after midnight."

Brian studied her downbent head, feeling suddenly as if he had wounded something small and defenseless. And the apology came unbidden. "I'm sorry, Rena," he said gently. "I guess I was thinking more of Long's reputation than of your . . . standards."

"You don't know what my standards are." Clearly Serena was unwilling to forgive so quickly. The misty gray eyes lifted briefly to meet his, and there was something sad in them.

"Don't look at me like that!" he exclaimed involuntarily.

She glanced around to summon the waiter. "Why don't we have breakfast, Brian," she suggested softly.

Since the waiter, no more immune than the rest of his kind to Serena's glances, was already at their table, pencil poised, Brian could do little but give his order after she had indicated her own choices. Then he stared at the top of her sable head for a few moments before he fully realized that he had irretrievably lost something by leaping to conclusions.

And it hurt, that loss. It hurt to realize that she would never again gaze at him innocently and confidingly, that she would now hesitate before reaching out to touch him. He had, with his accusation, lost a large portion of her trust.

Gone, he thought. Or was it? Serena was the most generous soul he had ever encountered, and perhaps . . . perhaps there would be no irretrievable loss.

Brian reached across the table to cover her slender hand with his own. "Rena"—his voice was very gentle—"I'm really sorry. After what you said last night, the only thing I was certain of was that you intended to marry Long. And I . . . I was angry. I'm so afraid you'll be hurt, and I don't want that to happen. I was worried about you, that's all. Will you forgive me?"

The misty gray eyes lifted to his again, and they were curiously shy this time. "I will. If . . . if you'll help me."

"Anything," he promised rashly, even as a little voice in his head warned him desperately. Those eyes, he thought, mesmerized, those damned eyes.

In the sweet, gentle voice that sounded like satin and could stop an army in its tracks, Serena said, "Teach me how to seduce a man."

She made it sound normal, he realized dimly. Ordinary. Not in the *least* dangerous. She made it sound matter-of-fact and innocent and entirely reasonable. She made it sound so reasonable, in fact, that Brian could not immediately think of a reason why he shouldn't do it.

Brian took a deep breath. "Rena," he said carefully, "there are some things you simply don't ask."

"Why not?"

He raked fingers through his hair. "Rena, you know damned well why not! You have to know! Asking me to teach you how to seduce a man is like—" Gazing into those inquiring eyes, Brian forgot what he was going to say. He cleared his throat and tried again. "You," he said very dryly, "are twenty-six. You've spent the better part of four years in Europe. Correct?"

Serena nodded, her brows still lifted inquiringly.

"You've certainly dated?" He waited for her nod, then nodded himself. "Then you have to know the effect you have on men. Most men, in fact."

"But you're my friend," she said, as if that made a difference.

At the end of his metaphorical rope, Brian fell back on brutal honesty. "Rena, if I taught you how to seduce a man, *I'd* be the man you seduced!"

Serena didn't respond for a few moments, since their waiter was busy placing their meal before them. Then, in her matter-of-fact way, she said cheerfully, "Well, that's all right with me, Brian. I don't think Josh would be pleased by a virgin in his bed anyway. So you can teach me how to seduce a man *and* please him in bed. And since we're friends, you won't be too rough with me, or—"

"*Serena!*"

She gazed at him, wide-eyed. Then those misty eyes grew even more misty, and her expression revealed how hurt she felt. "Oh. I see. I understand,

Brian, really I do. You don't have to say anything more."

"I don't think," he said from between gritted teeth, "that you understand at all, Rena."

"You don't want me. I understand."

"It isn't that." He swore roughly. "I'm responsible for you. How could I face Stuart after seducing his only daughter?"

"He wouldn't have to know," she offered, her tone one of anxious entreaty.

Brian stared at her for a long moment and then, very belatedly, remembered just who he was dealing with. A woman who had punched a policeman in the eye. A woman who had blithely jumped into the Mississippi River. A woman, he had learned, to his cost, who had taken the meaning of the phrase "iron hand in a velvet glove" to new and staggering heights.

He lifted his fork and began eating. Stalling for time.

"You *do* want me, don't you?" Serena asked with all the natural curiosity of a child. "I mean— the thought of seeing me naked isn't giving you the horrors, is it?"

Brian choked on his blueberry pancakes and reached hastily for his coffee. "Will you"—he wheezed—"for heaven's sake learn to give notice of loaded questions?"

"Well, *is* it giving you the horrors?"

Brian's principal reaction to the image her words had instantly provoked was hardly one of horror or revulsion, but he didn't think the breakfast table was quite the place to give vent to his emotions. Not, at least, in a restaurant.

"Serena," he said in a tone that had been compared by various of his friends to the sound of a saw biting into wood, "if you say another word not directly related to breakfast, I won't be responsible for my actions."

She stared at him for a moment, then cleared her throat with an odd little sound and addressed herself to eating the meal before her.

Brian ate automatically. His bland expression was the product of stern control. But his thoughts —and his imagination—refused to be governed. He had spent the past three weeks, he now realized, subconsciously reminding himself that Serena was, in the truest sense of the words, off limits. Not only was she the most enigmatic lady he'd ever met and completely out of his experience, but she was also the daughter of a man he greatly respected—and who trusted him implicitly.

Also, since her behavior had been as wayward, innocent, and troublesome as that of a child, he had been able to regard her, for the most part, in that light.

But since her incredible decision last night, Brian had found it impossible to think of her without remembering, however reluctantly, that she was very much a woman. And with that wall breached, he was painfully aware of just how attracted to her he was.

Attracted? he thought, with something akin to a mental groan. More than attracted. Fascinated. And she had only to smile at him to make him forget his name.

He didn't have to look at her to see the delicate face and mesmerizing eyes, or the slender body that her own words had stripped naked for him. Serena naked . . . God, he could see her that way so vividly that his entire body tensed and the blood began rushing hotly through his veins. His heart was pounding, his breathing roughening, and he fought the abrupt and primitive urge to snatch her up into his arms and . . .

Realization washed over him like an icy wave. Serena wanted Joshua Long. She had asked Brian to teach her how to seduce a man because she wanted Long. Asked him to teach her how to please a man because Long wouldn't want a virgin in his bed.

Virgin?

Brian felt his throat tighten, and a knot formed somewhere inside him. He pushed his plate away with controlled violence, staring at her downbent head with a gaze he knew to be savage.

Hell, didn't she know what she had asked of him?

He said nothing until the meal was finished, the check signed, and they rose simultaneously in unspoken agreement to leave the restaurant. Brian didn't dare take her arm or touch her in any way, but she remained silently beside him as they crossed the lobby and entered the elevator. And when they reached their floor, she unlocked the door to her room and preceded him inside.

Brian barely waited for the door to close behind him, but did manage to infuse his voice with dry mockery.

"So you've decided on strategy, Rena? You plan to learn how to tempt Long into your . . . web, didn't you call it?"

Serena sat down on the foot of her bed and stared up at him. Dressed in slacks and a silky blouse, she looked like a cross between temptress and teenager, and Brian was having a hard time keeping his urges leashed.

"I plan to learn," she answered matter-of-factly. "If you—someone—will teach me."

Brian paced over to the wide expanse of windows and stared out, unable to continue meeting her steady gaze. "And just how many lessons d'you plan to take, Rena?" he snapped. "How many nights? How many times would you sleep with me before going to him?"

"I suppose that would depend on how quickly I learned, wouldn't it?" she replied musingly, clearly undisturbed by the harsh questions.

He swung around to stare at her, his hands jammed in the pockets of his slacks. "Tell me something." He forced the words out and kept his feet rooted to the floor. "Has it occurred to you that it requires a certain amount of desire between *two* people? I assume you want Long, but you haven't said a damned word about wanting me."

Serena blinked, then said reasonably, "Well, I can hardly be sure of that, can I, Brian? You haven't even kissed me, for heaven's sake. But I'm sure an experienced man like you knows very well how to . . . turn a woman on. Don't you?" she added anxiously.

Brian knew that he should just leave her room. Immediately. He should have been able to treat this entire situation like the slightly amusing joke she probably intended it to be. He wanted to be able to do that. To laugh and speak lightly.

But he couldn't. He couldn't leave, and he couldn't treat this like a joke because it wasn't one to him. And because what she was offering him was something he wanted with every screaming nerve in his body.

There had never been a lack of women in Brian's life. He was attractive to women, he knew, and his personality was generally pleasant. Since he avoided long-term ties, his previous relationships could be summed up accurately as brief affairs. No strings, no promises, and no regrets when an affair was over.

So why, he wondered, was he hesitating now? Not, certainly, for the flimsy reasons he'd made up. Not because she was an enigma; that was, if anything, an inducement. And not because she was Stuart Jameson's daughter; she *was* of age, after all, and Stuart was hardly the type of genius who kept his head buried in the sand.

Brian gazed at Serena while she waited patiently for an answer to her question, and he tried to ignore the signals his body was sending urgently to his brain.

"I won't do it."

Where, he wondered, had those words come from?

She said nothing for a moment, her delicate face still; then she nodded and rose to her feet. "All right, Brian."

"What . . . will you do?" He couldn't leave it alone.

"I'll learn," she said simply.

"From whom?"

"That's my problem, Brian. Don't worry about it."

"Dammit, Serena . . ." He was standing in front of her before he'd even realized he had moved, and his hands were gripping her shoulders tightly. "You're going to be hurt, don't you realize that? And sleeping with one man to learn how to seduce another—my Lord, that's insane!"

She met his hot eyes steadily, unflinching. "Is it? Not in this day and age, Brian. I want to learn a . . . talent, if you will, because I need that talent. And since I know you don't want entanglements, it seemed to me that you'd be a good teacher."

"What makes you think I don't—"

"You told me," she interrupted calmly. "The day we met, in fact."

He couldn't recall that, but pressed on anyway. "That's beside the point, Rena."

"No, it's just the point. You haven't said, but you might want to sleep with me; however, you don't want more than that. And I want to learn how to please a man. So what's wrong with the idea of you and me having an affair? Josh is leaving tomorrow for about a week, but he's coming back, and he'll be here for at least two weeks after that. So we could—"

Obeying the urging of his body even as his mind continued to struggle, Brian pulled her suddenly against him. His hands slid down to the small of her back and then her hips, pulling her closer, nearly groaning aloud when her soft body curved instantly into the throbbing hardness of his own.

He shook his head slightly, bewildered, wondering at the power of this newly discovered desire for her. And when he felt her arms slide around his waist and her hands stroke his back lightly, he made a last desperate grab for reason.

"Rena," he said huskily, "there's nothing I want more than to lay you down on that bed and—" He broke off abruptly, his eyes closing as he fought for control; her body had moved against his, innocently and seductively, and he couldn't breathe for the wild need she'd ignited. When he forced his eyes open finally, he found hers gazing up at him with a wondering kind of pleasure.

"You don't have to kiss me, Brian," she murmured. "I know that I want you now. I knew as soon as I felt you against me."

Brian drew a single, harsh breath, then bent his head abruptly, his mouth finding hers. He couldn't have stopped himself even if he'd wanted to. And when her soft, cool lips warmed beneath his, opening to him, the last tendrils of reason vanished.

One hand slid up her spine to tangle in her thick, dark hair, holding her as close as possible while his lips slanted hungrily across hers. When his hand moved down her back to her waist, he could feel her move beneath the touch like a kitten pleasurably arching as it was stroked. That innocent movement, and the image it brought to mind, was just enough to jar him to his senses.

Struggling against a desire stronger than any he'd ever known, he managed to tear his mouth from hers and push her away from him. He was rougher than he'd meant to be, unbalancing her with the push, so that she sank down on the bed behind her.

He stared down at her for an endless moment, trying to catch his breath, trying to ignore the enticing image of Serena flushed and breathless, her eyes shimmering darkly with desire. Then, aware of how weak his determination actually was in the face of her unhidden response, he muttered a curse and strode from the room, slamming the door behind him.

Serena gazed at the closed door for a long time while her breathing gradually steadied. She stretched her slender body like a graceful cat. Odd, she thought, how different she felt physically. Every nerve in her body seemed to have been transformed. Alive . . . aware. Deliciously aware.

She lay back on the bed, staring at the ceiling, a faint frown between her brows. Complications, she thought. Nothing was ever simple, of course; the world was complicated, and people were complicated . . . and plans had to be complicated.

The situation might well have discouraged another woman, especially in the face of Brian's rejection, but not Serena. She enjoyed untangling things. Of course . . . sometimes it was necessary to tangle them even more before beginning to separate the various threads.

Brian attempted to work out his frustration on the hotel's tennis court, and succeeded at least in exhausting himself temporarily. After a shower he checked Serena's room, to find her gone, and anxiety started gnawing at him again as he went down to the lobby. A glance through the glass expanse fronting the lobby showed him a picture that stopped him in his tracks. Joshua Long stood by a black limousine, dressed for travel in a three-piece business suit. His head was bent attentively and a crooked smile softened his hard face as he spoke to Serena.

She had changed since the morning, Brian realized, coming to the depressing conclusion that although slacks were obviously good enough for himself, pursuit of Long demanded clingy silk dresses. And the green silk dress she wore certainly clung in all the right places . . . and a few wrong ones that aroused both Brian's protective impulses *and* his so-carefully banked desires.

He stood silently and waited, something in him tightening as he waited for the dark man to kiss Serena good-bye. And he did kiss her. Brian's blood pressure only rose a few degrees, however, since the kiss was clearly light and brief.

The limo pulled away and Serena came back inside the lobby, a faint smile curving her lips. She saw Brian and approached him, hiding the smile, but not quickly enough.

Brian felt savage.

"I hope you didn't wait to have lunch with me," she said cheerfully. "Josh had to go into town for a meeting this afternoon, and since he'll be gone until tonight—"

Gesturing impatiently, Brian cut her off. He really didn't want to hear about her lunch date. What he wanted—no, *had* to do was reestablish their earlier relationship. It was either that or, he knew, become the first lover in her life. A temporary lover. A teacher. And that understanding brought a bitter bile to his throat in a reaction he didn't care to probe.

"We have to talk," he told her.

"Well, we can go up—"

"No." Brian caught her elbow and led her toward the corner of the huge lobby that was sometimes a bar and always a place where people could sit and relax. He found a small grouping of chairs and love seats that was deserted, and gestured for Serena to sit down. "We aren't going to your room. Or mine."

Serena sat down, and watched as he took a chair at a right angle to her own. "Don't you trust yourself, Brian?"

For an instant, a single, fleeting moment, he caught a glimpse of the real Serena, the woman beneath all the innocent layers. It was in her eyes, something he'd never seen before but instinctively recognized. The look of a woman who knew exactly who and what she was: one hundred percent woman.

It made him dizzy, that look, and his desire lunged on its leash with a primitive strength. She was a woman in the prime of her life gazing at a man she wanted, and he could feel the knowledge blaze through his body like a river of fire.

And then the look was gone, and Serena's lovely face was tranquil again.

"You want to strangle me, I know," she elaborated. "Don't you trust yourself not to if we're alone?"

Brian knew—he *knew*—that Serena had deliberately changed the meaning of her question. And somehow he couldn't let her do that. He couldn't allow his recognition of that to pass unnoticed.

"No, I don't trust myself," he said evenly. "And you know it. You know damned well what you do to me."

She smiled a slow, fallen-angel smile that could, Brian realized glumly, put life into the Petrified Forest. "I *don't* know why you're fighting it," she said softly. "You act as if I've asked you to commit murder, Brian. I know you want me. I know I want you. So what's the problem?"

Brian didn't realize that his honest thoughts were going to surface until they did. And once they did, he didn't bother to halt them. "The problem is that it's too damned cold-blooded," he told her fiercely. "You decide you want to seduce Long into your bed and into a marriage, so you ask me to teach you! It's a cold, cut-and-dried plot, and sex should never be either."

Serena seemed not the least insulted at the unflattering picture he'd drawn of her intentions. Instead, she chuckled, honestly amused. "Considering your track record," she said cheerfully, "you're the last man I'd expect to make *that* objection, Brian."

"My track—" He stared at her. "Now, just what d'you mean by that?"

"Well, unlike Josh, you don't subsist on a steady diet of *blondes*, but I'd call it a steady diet. At least according to the papers."

Brian gritted his teeth and objected strongly. "I'm not cold-blooded about my relationships."

"Aren't you?" Her unwavering gaze was discon- certingly perceptive. "You know each . . . relation- ship . . . will end even before it begins. Isn't that a bit cold-blooded?"

He didn't quite know how to respond to that, and it bothered him. *Was* he cold-blooded? "No," he said finally. "It's simply a firm understanding of my own goals and an . . . an honest attitude toward adult relationships."

"Neat," she said approvingly, faintly mocking. "Covers all the bases nicely, I'd say." Before he could explode she added softly, "Now apply those same words to my situation."

It stopped him, but only for an instant. "That's—"

"Different? Is it, Brian? Is it really?"

Cornered, he fell back on a specific protest. "Rena, you're planning to use sex to get Long to the altar, and if that isn't cold-blooded, I don't know what is!"

"Oh, but I'm not!" Her smile was angelic. "I know sex is only a part of any relationship, and I'd certainly never use that as a weapon or re- ward. No, Brian, you misunderstand. I want to learn how to please Josh, that's all. I have another plan entirely for getting to the altar."

"What plan?" he demanded. When she only smiled seraphically, his frown deepened. "Rena, you aren't thinking of—"

"Trapping him? Of course not, Brian. I happen to believe a marriage should begin with two people—not three. I've taken precautions."

"You don't know what the word means!" he accused bitterly.

She leaned forward, one hand coming to rest

lightly on his knee with a touch he could feel through to his bones. "Stop worrying about me," she whispered. "Look, why don't you go on to California? I can finish the trip alone; Daddy will understand."

For a single instant, worried and angry, Brian considered that escape from the situation. But it wouldn't be an escape, and he knew it. He'd go crazy wondering if Serena had gotten in over her head—which he considered an ironclad certainty—with no one on the spot to help her. The thought of her reaching California after a successful "plan" had netted her a husband was something that was strangely hurtful to him, and he was unwilling to leave her to her plots and schemes.

"No," he said finally. "I signed on for the duration. I stay. I promised your father I'd look after you."

She sat back, her hand slowly trailing from his knee. "You'll stay, but you won't help me?"

"Serena, you—"

"I know you want me."

"That's beside the point," he managed to protest after drawing a deep, steadying breath.

She frowned briefly. "I see what it is. You prefer to do the chasing yourself."

"No, that isn't it! In fact, I'd be flattered . . . under normal circumstances. But this situation is hardly normal."

Serena didn't appear to be listening. Musingly, she said, "Maybe I should try seducing you."

Leashing his urges fiercely, Brian muttered, "*Lord*, you're dangerous!"

"It'd be good practice," she said, still musing.

"Serena, stop it! Just stop it, all right?"

Her smile was that of a mischievous sprite, and the gleam in her eyes definitely unnerved him. "I'll try seducing you completely against your will. How does that sound?"

"Like insanity!"

"You know what they say about resistance," she murmured. "It just makes the chase more determined. So you go ahead and run, Brian."

Almost to himself Brian muttered, "I thought I was assuming responsibility for a flighty kid whose worst fault was probably that she'd been spoiled rotten by her doting father. Instead I wind up with a beautiful, softhearted, ruthless woman who wants to practice the art of seduction on me so she can catch another man." He stared at her. "I must be out of my mind."

"Because you're going to let me do it?" she asked hopefully.

"*No*, I'm not going to let you do it!" he practically roared. Then he glanced around at a few startled faces and lowered his voice. "I must be out of my mind because I haven't tied you up, gagged you, and loaded you on the first plane to California!"

"You do have a temper, don't you?"

Since it was obviously a rhetorical question, Brian didn't bother to respond to it.

"I want you, Brian."

The soft words went through him like a hot knife, burning and hurting, and he found his eyes locked with her wistful gray ones. In that moment Brian understood fully and completely just how dangerous Serena Jameson really was.

Because nothing mattered. When she looked at him, nothing mattered but the ravenous need she could ignite with a few soft words and a glance.

"You want Long," he said hoarsely.

She smiled. "Right now I want you."

Brian rose to his feet, and every part of his body protested because he was going to leave her. "You don't need to learn a damn thing about seduction," he told her. "You've got it down pat!"

Three

Somewhat to Brian's surprise, Serena had no date with Long for dinner that night. Instead she knocked on his door and sweetly invited him to dine with her.

For a moment Brian was unable to answer, since he was busy wondering if it was a physical impossibility for the human heart to turn flips like a landed fish. When he was finally able to accept her invitation, he was unsurprised to hear the hoarseness of his own voice.

She was wearing a silver gown that had been designed with a creative flair and a total ignorance of the laws of gravity. It was backless to the flare of her hips, strapless, and the long skirt was slit up the side almost to her hip. Material that looked like nothing so much as a gossamer silver web—appropriate, he thought dimly—clung to her slender body to emphasize every curve, every hollow . . . and every breath she drew.

They were in the elevator descending to the

lobby when he had a very belated realization. "Dammit, you're starting!"

"Starting what, Brian?"

Another guest was in the elevator, and Brian only just managed not to blurt out what she was starting. Instead he contented himself with glaring at her briefly, then turning the glare on the stranger, who was staring at Serena. Encountering that stony gaze, the stranger hurriedly looked away.

Serena slipped her hand into the curve of his elbow and smiled up at him. "You have a nasty, suspicious mind," she told him placidly. "I'm just taking this opportunity to wear some of the gowns I bought in Paris."

"Is that what that is?" he questioned rather grimly. "A gown?"

"What did you think it was?"

"Ammunition." Under his breath, he muttered, "Why aren't you shooting at Long?"

"Brian, you're being cryptic. I'm not shooting at anybody at all."

Very conscious of her hand on his arm, Brian led the way through the lobby and into the restaurant. And he wasn't at all surprised to see heads turn and eyes widen as Serena preceded him to follow the waiter to their table. He also saw Long seated a few tables away from them. With a gorgeous blond companion.

Serena didn't appear to notice.

"You *are* shooting at him," Brian noted evenly the moment their waiter left. "Or at his date."

"I think I'll have the chicken," Serena murmured,

gazing at the menu thoughtfully. "It sounds good. What about you, Brian?"

He was still wondering at her motives. "Trying to make him jealous? Or the blonde rabid?"

"Why don't we have wine?"

"Serena." He waited until tranquil gray eyes lifted to his. "Dammit, which one of us is it tonight?"

She folded the menu and leaned forward slightly, her hand reaching to cover his clenched one. "Brian," she said softly, infusing his name with the sound and flavor of an endearment, "you're the only man in the room."

He knew—he *knew*—that she was doing it deliberately. But for some inscrutable reason that knowledge did nothing to slow his racing pulse. Carefully reclaiming his hand, he fixed his gaze on his menu and muttered, "You're a threat to mankind!"

Serena sat back and laughed, but made no comment. Instead she began to talk in the easy, companionable manner she had during the last three weeks. Brian, somewhat relieved, responded as best he could while striving to keep his gaze off her enticing décolletage.

A very sane and analytical part of his mind recognized that it was totally absurd for an experienced man of thirty-six to feel as callow as a smitten schoolboy in this woman's admittedly seductive presence. That same portion of his mind also questioned the validity of intelligence quotient tests; his I.Q. supposedly qualified him as highly intelligent.

Odd how quickly intelligence could desert a man. For her part Serena was her normal sweet, tranquil self. She made no further remarks Brian could have called suspicious, nor did she flirt with him. She talked quietly and casually, and it wasn't until dessert had been set before them that a warning bell rang in Brian's head.

"I'm sorry—what did you just say?" he asked cautiously.

Guileless eyes smiled at him. "I said that the Bishops are going into the city tomorrow afternoon, and I promised to watch the kids for them."

He took a deep breath. "Who are the Bishops, and how many kids did you promise to watch?"

"Brian, I'm sure you've seen the Bishops. They've been staying here as long as we have. They're the couple down the hall from us with the little boy and girl."

He remembered. He remembered two towheaded kids of about six and eight years old who looked like angels and behaved like creatures possessed by mischievous demons. The hotel staff already went in terror of the little monsters.

Those two . . . with Serena?

Brian looked down at the delicious-looking strawberry shortcake before him, and pushed the dish away with a sigh. He'd lost his appetite. He couldn't imagine why.

She giggled suddenly. "You don't have to help, Brian; I can take care of the kids myself. And it's only for a few hours."

"Wars," he noted, "have begun and ended in a few hours. Rena, do you *have* to do this?"

"I promised."

"Did the Bishops ask you?" He knew the answer.

"No, but I knew they hadn't had much chance

to be alone together. They tried one of the hotel sitters once, but haven't been able to get one since. They're always busy."

He saw the gleam of laughter in her eyes, and realized that Serena knew *why* the hotel sitters were all booked up when it came to the Bishop children. He sighed again. "Great. That's just great. If I have to bail you *and* two kids out of jail, I know I'll murder you."

"You worry too much." Serena had finished her own dessert under his unconsciously fascinated eye; she ate enough, he'd noticed, to feed three people, and never gained an ounce, that he could detect.

"I've been working on an ulcer," he agreed dryly. "For about three weeks now."

"Are you going to eat that?"

Silently he slid his dish across to her, and watched her dig in. "Where d'you put it?" he asked wonderingly, bemused.

Unoffended, Serena smiled at him. "Daddy says I have a peculiar metabolism. One of these days he plans to find out how it works so he can market the results and get rich."

"He's already rich."

"Richer, then. Besides, he wants to win the Nobel Prize, and he figures that'll do it."

"You never talk about your mother." He didn't know why he brought that up, except that he was curious.

Serena didn't respond for a moment, but then she pushed the half-eaten dessert aside and gazed at him steadily. "Mother was killed sixteen years ago."

He returned her gaze, sensing more from her even tone than from the words that there was a larger story behind her mother's death. His hand slid across the table to cover hers instinctively. "What happened?"

With her free hand Serena toyed with the stem of her wineglass. "It isn't a matter of public record," she said quietly. "It was listed as an accident. And it was that; they meant to get Daddy."

"What?" An icy finger traced his spine.

"Mother was going shopping. She left the house and drove Daddy's car; he'd had to take an emergency trip, so his car was there. She was just going shopping. We lived in the mountains, and the road into town was . . . one you had to be careful driving on. The police decided she'd just lost control on one of the curves. The car went over a cliff."

Brian's hand tightened on hers. "But you don't believe it was an accident?"

"Daddy was with a government think tank at the time. Since he was working on some . . . some very special projects, they sent out an investigative team of their own. The local police had determined that the car's brake line could have been severed in the crash, but the team didn't agree. Somebody had thought Daddy was going to be in that car, and only an emergency summons from his group had saved him.

"They didn't know if the group's security had been compromised or if it had been just a matter of someone's wanting to destroy a mind that couldn't be bought. Anyway, a cordon of security was thrown around Daddy and me."

"Did they find out who—?"

"No. Daddy was working in the field of physics then; it could have been any number of groups or organizations. Or countries." She sighed softly. "A couple of years later Daddy told them what they could do with his security clearance, and went to find work in the private sector. And he changed fields; it wasn't difficult for him. He went into engineering first, deciding it was a less-threatening area. Then he specialized in electrical engineering and computer technology. You know the rest."

Brian sat in silence for a moment, thinking of the man he'd known for two years and—he realized now—barely knew at all. A tall, still-handsome man with graying hair and mild gray eyes. A man who spoke little about himself and less about his past.

"I never knew," Brian murmured.

Serena's gaze was far away. "He doesn't talk about it. His love for Mother was very special. She'd been married before, very young, and her husband had died after only a few years. She and Daddy met a couple of years later. He loved her from the first. She was small and delicate, with the sweetest temper of anyone in the world. She was also wealthy—in her own right as well as by marriage. Daddy was working, making a name for himself, but not much money. It was another year before he got up the nerve to propose."

She laughed suddenly. "Can you imagine? Daddy nervous?"

"It does seem out of character." Brian smiled, but then, as the implications of what she'd told him sank in, he frowned. "Rena, even though he's no longer so much of a target—at least I assume he isn't—didn't Stuart worry about your touring Europe alone?"

Serena seemed lost in the past again. "Of course he worried. Still does. But neither one of us could stand being fenced in for long. I wanted to see Europe; he understood that. He'd made a point to keep me out of the public eye. Since I'm not a newsworthy person, I'm as safe as anyone is in these troubled times."

"Then why," Brian said evenly, "did Stuart insist on having someone accompany you home from England?"

Her smile died, and Serena's gaze dropped to the fingers still toying with her glass. After a long moment she said softly, "That project he's doing for you, Brian—if it's successful, it could change the way computers are designed and built. Yes?"

"Yes." He was beginning to understand, and that icy finger traced his spine again.

"Well, I'm sure your security is excellent; otherwise Daddy would have told you. But there are a lot of companies, a lot of big names, scrambling to get on top in the computer industry. The wave of the future. And a man of Daddy's reputation working for an innovative company like yours— well, it could start people thinking."

"Rena." He stared at her, waited until she met his gaze. "What *aren't* you telling me?"

Obviously choosing her words carefully, Serena said, "Daddy isn't worried about my physical safety, Brian. I mean, hiring bodyguards would have been ridiculous, aside from defeating the purpose by calling attention to me. What was needed was just a leisurely, unplanned trip with a very loose itinerary. And he wanted me to have company, to be on the safe side—"

"*Serena.*"

She sighed. "He got a few calls, Brian, that's all. A man's voice. The caller didn't say anything except the name of my hotel in Paris. Daddy alerted me; I changed hotels. The next day he got another call; my new hotel was named."

"My God, Serena—"

Her hand turned beneath his to clasp it firmly. "Brian, Daddy's lived with this kind of thing before. So have I. That caller just wanted him to know that I could be found if necessary. Daddy's gotten a few very lucrative offers in the last months; he thinks one of those who has made an offer is behind it. Someone wants him, and badly. And that someone is warning him to think carefully before he refuses the next offer."

Brian was no stranger to the concept of industrial spies, since he'd dealt with one or two in the ten years of his company's existence, but this kind of quiet, dangerous maneuvering was beyond his experience. "You should be somewhere safe," he muttered, his fingers tightening around hers.

"I am somewhere safe." She smiled at him. "I'm moving from place to place on the map, quietly and with no fanfare. In a rented car on anonymous highways and scenic roads off the beaten path. Never in any one place long enough to leave a trail. And, what's more important, I'm giving Daddy and his contacts time to follow *their* trail. When we reach California, Daddy will know who wants him so badly, and why. Once he knows, he'll be able to deal with it."

He didn't, Brian realized dimly, know Stuart Jameson *at all*.

"Why," he wanted to know, "wasn't I told this from the start?"

Serena hesitated. "I'm sorry, Brian, but that was my idea. I didn't know you, remember. And—to mangle a quote—I've *never* relied on the kindness of strangers. Or looked to strangers for protection. Daddy wanted it known you were traveling with me, and he sent you straight to London to give himself time to arrange things back here. When we reached New York we were registered at the hotel for four days—and left after two. They lost us after that; Daddy got a call placing me in New York, but they haven't mentioned me in the two calls since."

Shaking his head, Brian said incredulously, "Why *me*, for God's sake? If he wanted it known you had a companion, why not at least one bodyguard? One unobtrusive bodyguard, with an unobtrusive gun or two?"

"I don't like guns," Serena said firmly. "And no matter *how* unobtrusive he tries to be, a bodyguard always *looks* like a bodyguard. And that provokes questions. 'Why on earth d'you suppose the little lady needs a watchdog? Maybe she's somebody the local paper would pay a few dollars to find out about.' And so on. I've seen it happen. This way, all anyone knows is that I'm traveling with a very handsome man, important enough to garner a few front-page headlines, whom my father happens to work for."

Then, a suddenly mischievous glint in her eyes, she added blandly, "A man, moreover, who's well known for his ability to take care of himself, and anyone else who rears a troublesome head. He's athletic, has a black belt in karate, and is a licensed pilot capable of flying any and all private aircraft. He earned a few marksman's medals in the army, where he distinguished himself remarkably for peacetime, by the way."

Brian had a dim feeling his mouth was hanging open.

"His favorite color is blue," Serena went on gently, "he drinks Scotch but prefers wine, takes his coffee black and strong, and loves Italian food and semiclassical music. He keeps his very nice condo neat without benefit of anything but once-a-week help, the leaning toward neatness possibly a holdover from the army but more likely the result of being raised by a Scots-Irish mother and a German-English father, who is presently a retired general who does the Sunday *Times* crossword in an hour *flat.*"

"Serena—"

"Their paragon of a son," she finished innocently, "is also adept at difficult crossword puzzles —and other kinds of puzzles—since he boasts an I.Q. that ranks him as something of a minor genius."

"Minor—" He stared at her. "What's your I.Q.?" he demanded abruptly.

"Same as yours," she murmured.

Brian drew a deep, slow breath. "D'you mind telling me," he managed to ask politely, "just where

you got all that information about me? I don't
recall being asked to fill out a questionnaire."

"Oh, here and there."

"That's no answer."

"I asked Daddy."

"Stuart's never been to my condo, and he doesn't
know my favorite color. Try again."

"Daddy. Seriously, Brian. He knows an awful
lot that he doesn't *seem* to know. And a man in
his position, well . . . he found out all he could
about you before he ever signed on; it's habit,
after all these years."

Brian was trying manfully to grapple with all
the surprising, disturbing information that had
capped a deceptively peaceful meal. "Let me get
this straight. Person or persons unknown intend
to hire your father away from my company by fair
means or foul. The 'fair' includes dollars on a
scale I don't want to ask about; the 'foul' includes
possible kidnapping and/or bodily harm threatening yourself. Right so far?"

"That was just lovely. You do have a way with
words," she said admiringly.

Brian ignored the plaudits. "In an attempt to
remove you from circulation, your father has sent
you on a cross-country jaunt with me as watchdog, while he busily, heaven only knows *how*,
tracks down these unknown people."

"That sums it up nicely."

"And—*and*—while all this is going on, while
you are presumably safest moving from place to
place, and while your father and his mysterious
'contacts' attempt to track down these equally mysterious people, while I'm being led by the nose

down a blind alley filled with thugs, for all I know—" Under stress, Brian lost track of his sentence and hastily backed up to the point. "While all this is going on, you're planning to stay here in Denver for at least three weeks? Stay in one place? The worst thing you could possibly do at the moment?"

"I thought I would," she confirmed cheerfully.

Brian made a sound indicative of despair.

"Why don't we walk in the garden?" she suggested.

"You'll catch your death in that gown," he retorted.

"I never catch cold."

"Who said anything about a cold?" he muttered, signing the check and then following behind as Serena glided—there was no other description for the way she walked—from the restaurant. As they passed Long and his blond companion, Brian saw the other man shoot Serena a quizzical look, eyebrow lifted and amusement gleaming in his eyes; since Brian was behind Serena, he couldn't see her response. But she had probably, he thought sourly, given Long a come-hither look to end them all.

Brian was feeling somewhat put-upon. Being an honest man, he acknowledged inwardly that he was also feeling angry, sorely abused, bewildered, slightly anxious over the possibility of a kidnapping in the near future, and jealous. And he wanted Serena Jameson until he couldn't think straight *anyway.*

He was hardly in the mood for a quiet stroll through a discreetly lighted garden. But when Serena slipped her hand beneath his arm and when he looked down at the top of her sable head and at the silver gown she hadn't bothered to cover with a wrap, he couldn't seem to form a protest.

"Why is it," she asked thoughtfully, "that we always seem to fight in restaurants? Have you noticed?"

"We weren't fighting. I was just trying to hold on to my sanity," he corrected.

They walked slowly in silence for a few moments. Then Serena stopped, turning to gaze up at him almost as if she'd never seen him before. The whitewashing moonlight and shrubbery lighting might have been deceptive, but she looked both pale and oddly uncertain. And she spoke with unusual seriousness. "Go back to California, Brian."

He was more than a little startled, since her voice sounded shaky, and very small. He saw an expression on her delicate face he'd never seen before: a strange, masked vulnerability.

She looked up at him, her expression naked. "Go back," she repeated softly. "I'll be all right here. Daddy said they were closing in on whoever it is. I'm not in any danger now. And you've put up with me long enough."

"I told you." He found his hands lifting to her bare, tanned shoulders. "I'm in for the duration."

"You said that," she agreed wryly. "But you didn't know then what the duration entailed. You deserve combat pay, Brian. Even for just this far, these last weeks. I've put you through hell." She laughed shakily. "I've said and done ridiculous things, I know. Oh, I know." Her chin dropped, and there was something bewildered and child-like in the gesture. "I get things all tangled and confused. Sometimes," she confessed softly, "I do it deliberately. But not always."

"Rena—"

She cut him off, speaking rapidly, her voice suddenly taut. "Dammit, I'm trying to warn you. I play tricks, Brian. I plot and I scheme—and I always get my own way. You don't know—"

"I know," he interrupted gently, "that you're kind and softhearted and generous. I know that, Rena."

Her chin lifted and her gray eyes shimmered wetly. "You're not *listening* to me!"

He was, but more than that, he was looking at her. Looking at her and wondering if the dredged-up memories of her mother and her mother's violent death had opened the wound he saw hurting in her eyes. Brian had felt protective impulses toward her before, but those impulses had always been tinged with exasperation. Not this time, not now.

He wanted to draw her into his arms and hold her, protect her. And that feeling swirled oddly among the tendrils of the desire he felt for her, confusing him with the tenderness both combined to produce. He'd never felt this way before.

His hands lifted to frame her face warmly. "Why are you telling me this now, Rena?" he asked gently, gazing into her wet, shadowy eyes. "Because you feel guilty that I was named watchdog without being told about it? Is that it? Because if that is it, you may as well shut up. I'm not leaving you."

Her hard voice contrasted sharply with the wet misery in her eyes. "I'm after Josh, remember? You'll just get in my way, Brian!"

He might have been hurt or angered by the words, but he was concentrating on trying to understand what reasoning lay behind them. Serena was suddenly wearing a new hat, one he'd never seen or even suspected she owned before, and it intrigued him. Was it deliberate? Somehow he didn't think so.

"I'm not leaving you, Rena." He found a smile. "I couldn't if I wanted to. And I don't want to."

Her eyes closed briefly, and she spoke in an oddly suspended voice. "What would you say if I told you I loved you?"

He felt his heart stop, then begin pounding against his ribs. "I'd say: then why're you after Long?"

"Maybe you'd better think about that, Brian." Her arms went around his waist beneath his jacket, and her warm body pressed against his. "Maybe you'd better think about it."

He couldn't think about anything except the touch of her, the feeling of her against him. And the sight of those enigmatic gray eyes gleaming up at him filled his vision. If his body had been stone, he might have resisted her; being human, he just couldn't.

"Rena . . ." His head bent, his lips seeking and finding hers in a touch that was gentle only for an instant. Her response was immediate, total; she became a slender flame that scorched him until every nerve ending shrieked awareness. He felt the smooth skin of her back beneath his hands and the thud of her heart against his chest, and his mind reeled with a wave of hot, savage desire. Her lips returned his kiss fiercely, as hungry as his own, as desperate.

And then, wildly, she wrenched away from him. There was something pagan about her as she stood staring up at him, breasts heaving and eyes flashing.

"I won't lose control," she gasped out, anger and bewilderment filling her voice. "Damn you, I won't lose control of this!" And then she was gone, disappearing around a bend in the path leading back to the building.

Brian stood where she'd left him, his body taut and his mind bewildered. After a while, slowly, he started back to the building. Thinking. Wondering.

Serena was still moving quickly, though no longer running, when she reached the lobby. And when she met Josh as he was coming back into the hotel, her voice emerged as brittle as fragile crystal.

"What? You mean you didn't even invite her to stay the night? Josh, I'm surprised at you!"

"Not every evening," he said dryly, "has to end in a bedroom." He looked down at her for a moment, then caught one of her cold hands and tucked it into the crook of his arm. "Come on. I'll walk you up to your room."

"Thanks." She stared straight ahead, not speaking, while they went up in the elevator. Still in silence she unlocked her door before glancing up at him.

"How about a nightcap?" he asked quietly.

Serena nodded, preceding him into the room and closing the door behind them. While he wandered over to the window and stared silently out, she fixed two drinks at the compact bar. She didn't ask what he wanted, but automatically prepared straight Scotch for them both. Then she handed him a glass and sank down on the foot of the bed to swallow half her drink.

Still gazing out the window, Josh said softly, "The watchdog has teeth, eh?"

Serena gazed at her glass without answering.

Josh crossed to half sit on the low dresser in front of her. "Serena?"

Reluctantly, wryly, she met his steady gaze.

"You caught a tiger by the tail this time, didn't you?"

Four

Serena grimaced. "The laugh's on me," she said, her voice low. "Go ahead, Josh; you said you would laugh."

"When you got tangled in one of your own plots?" He looked at her, grave. "It's odd, but I don't seem to find it very funny. What happened?"

Serena finished her drink and stared at the empty glass. "I don't know. He asked about Mother during dinner, and I told him all that. I also told him the rest."

"About Stuart's troubles?"

"Yes."

"How'd he take it?"

"He was angry. Worried." She smiled a little. "Feeling a bit ill-used, I think."

"Can't blame him for that."

"No." She sighed, then added abruptly, "I told him . . . In the garden I told him to go back to California."

Josh's rather hard blue eyes sharpened. "That

55

doesn't sound like you," he commented, thoughtful. "Did Ashford decide to leave?"

"No. Oh, no. He's an honorable man, you know. He promised Daddy, and he's staying."

"You think that's his reasoning?" Josh asked mildly. "That he's just keeping a promise?"

"Well, he isn't staying for love of me," she retorted bitterly. "Dammit, he's got more walls than you have."

"Which explains, I take it, why you decided on this very tangled web you have us all enmeshed in?"

Serena gestured helplessly with one slender hand. "It seemed like a good idea at the time." She brooded silently for a moment, then looked up to find him watching her intently. "It did seem that way, Josh. After three weeks I knew— Well, I knew. But it was painfully obvious he thought of me as some troublesome kid with half a brain. *Kid!*" she finished incredulously.

"I don't think," Josh commented, "anyone else has treated you as a kid since you were seven. Troublesome, yes. A kid, no."

"Well, I did give him a lot of trouble," she said fairly. "I mean, I really pulled out the stops and chewed the scenery. But I just wanted to make sure he could handle it. When I get like that, I mean."

"And did he handle it?"

"Oh, he handled it beautifully. Even when he yelled at me, he didn't really lose his temper." Smiling suddenly, she added, "But you should have seen his face when he bailed me out of jail!"

"You are a difficult woman," Josh observed judiciously.

"I know." She sighed.

After a few moments of silence—brooding, on Serena's part—Josh spoke again. "How is the jealousy ploy working?"

Serena looked at him. "I wish I knew."

"What?" He laughed. "You mean he isn't a victim of the green-eyed monster, and isn't filled with visions of decking me for corrupting the innocent?"

"I think he's wanted to deck you once or twice," she answered thoughtfully. "But that's probably just his sense of responsibility working overtime."

"No green-eyed monster, though?"

She was silent for a moment. "I don't think so. He's attracted. I don't have to tell you about chemistry."

"No," Josh said very dryly. "You don't have to tell me about that."

"Yes, well . . . He got quite stiff about the whole situation when I asked him to teach me how to seduce you, and—"

"When you asked him what?"

Serena avoided his incredulous stare. "It seemed like a good idea. At the time."

Josh looked plaintively toward the heavens, wondering vaguely if Brian Ashford had noticed how men invariably tended to do that in Serena's presence. Finally he returned his gaze to her. "My dear Serena," he said politely, "you need a man who'll beat you silly. Twice a day."

She studied his expression thoughtfully. "Funny, but Brian reacted in a similar way. Different words, though. And when I just happened to mention I'd never slept with a man before, he—"

Josh closed his eyes and swore solemnly for several long moments.

"I shouldn't have told him that?" she ventured.

"I think I'll call Stuart," Josh murmured. "It's way past time to have you committed."

"Josh—"

"Serena," he interrupted gently, looking at her with the despairing gaze of a man who *knows* explanations are pointless, "you've just told the man you'd like him to be your first lover, with the express intention of learning how to become another man's lover. Now, don't you think that just *might* have bothered him a little?"

She reflected for a moment, then looked at him uncertainly. "I know it bothered him. He said it sounded cold-blooded, and that sex should never be that."

"To which you replied?"

"Well, I drew a comparison with his life. Short-term relationships he *knew* would be nothing more from the beginning. He defended that, just as I thought he would, by saying it was an understanding of adult relationships and his own goals. I told him to apply those words to me."

Josh sighed. "Serena—"

"I know, I know! It's different. You want to tell me *how* it's different?"

"You're using him," Josh answered promptly. "Or at least it seems that way to him."

After a moment Serena sighed, and gestured bewilderedly. "And I'm tangled in my own damned plot! Josh, when he said he wouldn't teach me, I wasn't worried. He—well, I knew he wanted me. But when we were in the garden, something happened. And I don't know what it was. I couldn't think. I looked at him, and . . . and I just couldn't think. That was when I told him to go back to California. And I asked him what he'd say if I told him I loved him."

"What *did* he say?"

"He asked why I was after you, then. I told him he should think about it." She looked at Josh confusedly. "Why did I do that?" She felt the same bewilderment she'd felt then, the same panicky sensation of having lost the threads of her plot.

Josh leaned forward, elbows resting on his knees, and gazed at her quietly. "You are tangled, aren't you?"

Serena shrugged helplessly. "I just—dammit, I as good as told him he was the one I wanted. And now I want to run. I want to get away from him. I'm *afraid!* I don't know why, but I am."

Josh nodded, as if to confirm some private deduction. "You looked scared in the lobby; I thought something like that had happened. I thought maybe it *would* happen, in fact."

"How could you think it'd happen?"

He smiled a little. "You forget. I've watched you work. You control things, Rena. People. You never hurt anyone, and I've often suspected you're perceptive enough to guide them in directions they want to go anyway. But you're always in control. Maybe even detached."

Serena looked at him, anxious. "I care about people."

"I know you do," he said instantly. "In fact, you

care more about people than anyone else I know. And that, plus the brains you inherited, makes for a somewhat Byzantine personality." He smiled again. "Fascinating to watch. The point is, though, that you've never plotted for yourself. Never used any kind of scheme to get something *you* wanted. This time you did."

"And so?"

"And so you couldn't be detached from this one. Your own feelings got in the way. Any poet, honey, would be delighted to tell you what happens when a person falls in love. The mind goes first, I'm told."

"I can't control," she said slowly, hollowly.

Josh nodded confirmation. "That's what I'd say. In fact, I've been waiting to see if that would happen. If you could stick to your neat little plot, control Ashford and yourself, then it wouldn't be the real thing. It would be just what Ashford thought it—cold-blooded. But it isn't that. Not now. Your emotions are in control now, and no one ever claimed emotions were logical."

Serena stared at him. "Josh, d'you have to leave the hotel?"

He got to his feet, setting aside his glass, and smiled down at her. "I won't be your buffer, you know," he told her quietly. "I was willing to go along with you on the jealousy bit—mainly because I knew it probably wouldn't work. But you've pretty much shot that down anyway. You've very likely confused the hell out of Ashford, but I doubt he'll take it seriously if you go on making sheep's eyes at me. No, honey, you're on your own now."

"So you're leaving?"

He nodded. "In the morning."

Shrewd gray eyes met his for a moment, and Serena said dryly, "But you won't go far, not out of town."

For the first time Josh seemed uncomfortable. "I told you I had business—"

"And I know what kind of business." She laughed, half amused and half irritated. "Daddy played innocent too; he acted surprised you were in Denver. But it occurred to me it was just a bit too pat that you were at this hotel. I had told him earlier where we'd be staying; I knew the phone was safe. He called you in, didn't he? Reinforcement."

Josh sighed and folded his arms across a broad chest; he gazed down at her ruefully. "He just wanted me to be handy, Rena. In case. That's all."

She looked at him for a long moment, then said steadily, "This isn't a good time for my plots, is it? Daddy's worried."

Josh hesitated, but he knew Serena too well to dissemble. "He's worried. *I'm* worried. Stuart's hit solid walls in trying to find out who's behind the threats, and it looks like they've traced you as far as Wichita."

For the first time since the whole thing started, Serena felt a chill. "Questions at our hotel there?"

He nodded. "Stuart pulled some strings; according to all records, you and Ashford left Denver last night on a flight to Phoenix. With any luck, they'll buy that. The rental car could be anywhere, including on the road, being used as a decoy."

She squared her shoulders unconsciously. "So you're leaving this hotel, but staying nearby. In case."

"If you leave the hotel for any reason," he instructed firmly, "call me first." Removing a business card from his pocket, he handed it to her. "Number's on the back. And you'd better tell Ashford it's more serious than we thought."

Serena's smile was a little painful. "Just when I wanted to run, I have to pull up the drawbridge and stay put. Great."

"That's not all." He grimaced slightly at her sharp look. "I know you won't like this—"

"A real watchdog." She spoke grimly.

"Sorry, Rena. Stuart's orders. The man's a P.I. with plenty of security experience. He'll just keep an eye on the comings and goings here at the hotel. You won't even know he's around."

"Want to bet?"

He grinned faintly. "Okay, so maybe *you'll* know he's around. But it's strictly low profile; he won't hover over you with one hand ready to reach for his gun. I promise."

"Brian's just going to love all this," Serena muttered.

"You'd better tell him. All of it."

"Who you are, you mean?" Her expression was wary. "I'm not so sure I want to do that just yet."

"When did you originally plan to tell him?" he asked, curious.

Serena reflected. "First anniversary?" she offered ruefully.

He chuckled softly. "You know, for someone whose plots are generally successful, you don't plan ahead, do you?"

She looked up at him, the same masked vulnerability Brian had seen in the garden again tightening her face. "Not this time. It looks like I haven't done anything right this time. Josh, he's going to hate me! And he won't leave, not when he finds out it's more serious. He'll stay with me—and he'll hate me!"

Josh reached for her hands, drawing her to her feet. "Somehow I doubt that, Rena. It'd take a very hard and vindictive man to hate you, and I don't think Ashford's that."

She sighed and sent him a humorous glance. "You think more of him than he thinks of you. I believe 'rake' was the kindest word he used."

Josh grinned, the tough, handsome face softening amazingly. "His judgment's faulty where I'm concerned. I'm the villain of the piece, after all."

Serena began looking thoughtful. "Maybe I can use that somehow. Until I tell him the truth, I mean. Sometimes tangling a problem even more is the way to untangle it."

Josh was unsurprised, yet still he winced. "I was afraid you were going to say that. Look, Rena, I don't mind—very much—being window dressing for you. But I'll be damned if I'll meekly let Ashford knock me into next week. Which, until he's figured you out or learns the truth, he's very likely to do."

"If you hit him I'll never forgive you," she said instantly.

"There was a humorous gleam in his blue eyes. "Honey, if Ashford slugs me—"

"Please, Josh! You both know karate; if one of you doesn't back down, you'll both get hurt!"

Josh lifted his eyes heavenward. Then he sighed.

"All right. But he could probably use a good fight. Dissipates tension, you know."

Serena ignored the information. "Promise?"

"I promise," he agreed dryly. "Besides—from the look of him, if he decks me I'll be awhile getting back up. What does he eat for breakfast anyway, nails?"

She was gazing at him, obviously occupied by thoughts of her own. "How's your evil-rake-bent-on-seduction laugh?" she asked suddenly.

Josh laughed, but it was a sound of pure amusement.

"That won't do!" she told him, mildly cross.

"Honey," he said, still laughing, "don't ask me to play an impossible part, or Ashford'll smell a rat!"

"From what I've heard, it isn't at all an impossible part for you. Not evil, maybe, but you've been bent on seduction for years." She looked at him curiously. "Why blondes?"

"I avoid brunettes." He eyed her dark hair thoughtfully. "Can't imagine why."

"It isn't because of me," she said scoffingly.

Josh was already regretting his careless comment, and only shrugged. Truth to tell, it wasn't because of Serena that he avoided brunettes, but he had no intention of explaining the matter to her. An amazing woman, Serena, with a heart of gold . . . and if she knew the truth about his weakness she was perfectly capable of using that knowledge ruthlessly.

"Look," he said, "why not just be honest with him? It's been known to work."

She looked at him and shook her head a little.

"I told you. He has more guards than you have, and you can't fight through walls. I couldn't think of a way over them or around them, so I decided to go through them any way I could. When we face each other on the same side of those walls, then I'll be honest."

After a moment Josh said, "And what if he decides a fling was enough? To get through his walls you'll have to drop your own. There won't be anything for you to hide behind, Rena."

"I know." She squeezed his hand and smiled in a way Brian wouldn't have recognized, because it was entirely vulnerable and a little scared. "That's . . . that's a chance I have to take."

"He could hurt you."

"Funny. He said the same about you."

"I believe it." Josh sighed. "In fact, if you have your way about it, people are going to start using my reputation to frighten children with," he commented sadly. "Clearly I'm a rotten human being."

She looked up at him for a moment, her lips twisting. "I'm using you, too, huh?"

"Only because I let you," he told her gently. "Rena, you're too softhearted to make people do what they don't want to do. It's your saving grace, I think."

"Am I as terrible as I sound?" she wanted to know in a small voice.

He grinned at her. "No. You're worse!"

Serena shook her head slowly.

"Now. Seriously," Josh said, "I think it's time you put the tricks aside for a while, don't you?"

She was silent for a long moment, then smiled

slowly. Oddly. "Yes. I'll tell Brian the truth. The whole truth."

"You're still plotting!" Josh accused with the acute perception of experience.

Serena looked at him guilelessly. "I'll tell him the truth," she repeated.

"What truth?" Josh demanded suspiciously.

Obediently she said, "I'll tell him what's going on with Daddy. And I'll explain all about your being window dressing because I wanted to make him jealous." She smiled. "And I'll explain why I wanted to make him jealous."

"You will?" He was still suspicious. He knew Serena.

"Well, what else can I do?" she asked reasonably. "I've as good as told him how I feel. Why not just be honest?"

Josh could tell she was up to something, but he couldn't follow her reasoning. It wasn't surprising; he couldn't follow her tortuous reasoning half the time, and scared himself the rest of the time when he *could* follow her reasoning. "You'll tell him the whole truth?"

"And nothing but the truth," she said, solemn. "I swear."

"I wish," he said despairingly, "that made me feel better." He wasn't surprised at her changes of mood since he'd entered her room tonight, and he wasn't entirely surprised that she'd decided to confess the truth to Ashford. What surprised him was how quickly she'd given in.

"Why?" he demanded suddenly, staring at her. "Why do you want to tell him the truth now?"

Since there had always been complete honesty

between them, Serena answered honestly. "I just don't want to trick him anymore." Her smile was shaky. "I've been thinking about what happened in the garden—and that's what it was. I looked at him and I couldn't stand tricking him. So I'll tell him the truth."

Startled, Josh realized then that there was something about Serena that *was* guileless, something innocent. She was, he saw in astonishment, utterly and completely vulnerable—under all those plotting, scheming layers.

And if he, with considerably more than three weeks' experience of her, had been deceived into thinking her far from vulnerable, then what would Brian Ashford believe?

"All your walls down," Josh murmured. He felt a little grim, and more than a little awed. That Serena, with years of cheerful plotting and scheming at her back, should cave in abruptly because she loved a man was incredible.

Serena deciphered the expression on his lean face with no trouble. "Time to grow up," she said softly. "I can't control everything, can I, Josh? I'm not even sure I can control me. Now. With him. I think I knew that even when I said I'd wait for his walls to fall before I was honest with him."

After a moment Josh sighed. "I wish I could make it easier for you, Rena—at least to the extent of removing all these . . . outside influences. It'll be hard enough for you to deal with yourself and Ashford without having to be on guard all the time. But I can't do anything about that." He reflected for a moment, then nodded decisively.

"Except stay here at the hotel and keep an eye out myself."

"You planned to leave tomorrow," she reminded him.

"That was the original idea," he agreed. "Partly because you wanted me here only a few days for the jealousy ploy, and partly because I was going to do a little snooping to find out if Stuart's would-be employers had actually lost you or were just keeping quiet about having found you."

"Did Daddy want you here at the hotel?"

"He said he'd feel better if I were. So I'll stay. Especially since you're going to tell Ashford the truth." Josh glanced at his watch, and added firmly, "Tonight."

She grimaced, and confessed ruefully, "I was hoping to use your absence for a little breathing room."

"You said you were going to be honest with him."

"Yes. But do I have to bare my soul *tonight*?"

Josh grinned at her. "You'll feel better with it all behind you. You know what they say about confession being good for the soul."

"He's going to kill me," she said darkly.

"You are," Josh told her, "dressed to kill—not dressed to *be* killed. I think Ashford will know the difference."

She sighed. "All right. I'll tell him. If he's speaking to me. Maybe he's not speaking to me," she added hopefully.

"Never put off till tomorrow. I'll knock on his door as I pass and tell him you want to see him."

"Are you sure you want to do that? The two of

you haven't even been introduced. Besides, Josh, he thinks you're the villain—remember? He could—"

"He's a rational man, Rena. I'll just tell him you want to see him."

"Why don't I just go to his room—"

"Nothing's going to happen!"

Brian was in a very peculiar mood. After hearing about the men who might be on Serena's trail, he was anxious, and after the scene in the garden he was more than slightly confused. Three weeks of Serena's company had taken their toll on his nerves when they'd arrived in Denver; after the surprises here, he knew himself to be badly in need of time to stop and think things through.

Though generally a controlled and quiet man, Brian had a considerable temper, and the physical expertise to cause a respectable amount of havoc if he lost control; he was near the edge now, he knew. He needed an outlet for the various kinds of frustrations building inside him.

He paced his room, jacket and tie cast aside, sleeves rolled up. Restless. He couldn't get a handle on Serena's sudden turnabout; her motivations eluded him.

So when he answered the firm knock at his door and found Joshua Long standing there, he felt an abrupt inclination to give in to at least one of his frustrations.

And his temper took over.

As if he were someone else, he felt his face assume a mildly quizzical expression, felt himself step back and gesture for the other man to enter the room. Long seemed surprised, but he came in. Brian wondered vaguely why there seemed to be a red veil between himself and his visitor.

Josh could have explained that. He turned, and had only a moment to note that red haze. And in that instant he recognized sheer, flaming temper in the other man's eyes, and thought fleetingly and wistfully of his confident words to Serena. He barely had time to finish the thought.

"If we break the furniture," Brian said calmly, "I'll pay for it." That was his only warning.

Joshua Long remained exactly as he'd fallen, except that he sat up. Working his jaw gingerly with one long-fingered hand, he stared up at Brian expressionlessly. "Contrary to popular opinion," he said, mildly under the circumstances, "the boardroom isn't the only place I tend to come out swinging. However . . ."

Brian, although he definitely felt better, was rather surprised at himself, since he couldn't remember ever slugging another man who hadn't provoked him physically. He met that steely blue stare—and every male instinct he could lay claim to told him that Long wanted badly to come *up* swinging this time. He *really* wanted to. But he sat there and rubbed his jaw, and somehow managed not to lose a single iota of dignity.

"Serena owes me for this," Long said wryly.

"Get up," Brian told him.

"I'd love to," Josh responded cordially. "I could use a good fight. Unfortunately, I promised Rena I'd be the one to back down if you started a fight." He frowned, but there was sudden laughter in his eyes. "And you did start it. Barely gave me time to turn around, in fact. Not cricket at all."

Absurdly, Brian didn't know whether to laugh and apologize or to yank Long up by his lapels and get the fight going in earnest. Lacking a stronger incentive, he gave in to temper again, verbally. "Look, I said get up, you—"

Long raised a hasty hand. "I really think," he said gravely, "you shouldn't say anything else until you've talked to Rena. Otherwise you'll want to apologize later for what you're about to say, and that'll put the both of us in a damned uncomfortable position."

Temper fled as Brian felt a bone-deep chill. The other man's words, he thought, could only mean . . .

Josh Long climbed to his feet, eyeing Brian warily. Absently straightening his tie he said, "And I think you're on the wrong track again. Talk to Serena, will you? She's in her room now, waiting to find out if you're still speaking to her."

In a kind of daze Brian followed him out into the hall. Josh gave him a last look, a faintly musing, sympathetic look, seemed about to speak, then merely shook his head and strode toward the elevators.

Brian found himself in front of Serena's door. He stared at it for a long moment, then squared his shoulders, braced himself, and knocked. She opened the door, quiet, subdued, and stepped back for him to enter.

"Did . . . did Josh tell you?"

"He said you wanted to talk." Brian heard his

strained, harsh tone of voice, and wished he could sound as if he didn't care.

"Would you like a drink?" She was gazing at him, a little puzzled and wary.

Brian shoved his hands into the pockets of his slacks and forced himself to meet her gaze without flinching. "No. Thanks. You have something to tell me?"

For some reason Serena felt that he wouldn't want to sit down, either. She leaned a hip against the low dresser and crossed her arms over her breasts. "Um, as a matter of fact, I do. Several things." She felt nervous and acutely uneasy; she'd been right to think he was going to hate her after this. Obviously he could barely stand to be in the same room with her now. And he looked so . . . grim.

She felt miserable, and her whole body hurt.

"I'm listening," he said flatly.

Serena winced. "Josh didn't tell you anything?" she ventured to ask.

Brian seemed to grit his teeth. "Just that you wanted to talk to me."

So talk! He didn't say it, but it vibrated in the air between them, impatient and harsh.

Almost inaudibly she murmured, "Daddy said you could be a hard man when you wanted to. I should have paid attention."

"Serena—"

"All right." She stared at him, bracing herself inwardly. "I told you . . . tonight in the garden I told you that I play tricks. I do, Brian. And . . . and I played a lousy trick on you."

Brian managed a laugh that sounded like a

snarl. "Don't tell me. Let me guess. You used me to make Long jealous."

Serena blinked. "No. The other way around."

A new tension stole into Brian, and his earlier confusion settled back onto his shoulders. "What?"

"I was using Josh, hoping to make you jealous," she confessed in a small voice. "I was lying when I implied that I wanted to marry him." Wary of his stunned expression, Serena rushed on. "You seemed so conscious that I was Stuart Jameson's daughter, I didn't think you really saw me except as some troublesome kid. *Kid!*" That rankled. "So I decided to prove to you I was a woman. It seemed like a good idea at the time," she finished desperately, very conscious of the oft-repeated refrain of her childhood.

Brian felt strangely suspended; he couldn't seem to grasp what she was telling him. "You knew Long before he came here to the hotel?"

Serena nodded.

"How long have you known him?"

Serena cleared her throat carefully. "I've known him all my life." Judging by his expression, she realized further clarification was needed. "I told you my mother had a previous marriage. Well, Josh is the sole product of that marriage."

"He's your half brother?" Brian asked faintly.

Hoping to avoid being strangled—there was a definite possibility of that, she was afraid—she hastily clarified a bit more. "Josh's father was a very wealthy man; he left most of his estate in trust for his son. Until Josh came of age, his uncle had control of the various businesses, and Josh spent a lot of time with his aunt and uncle in the East. He and Daddy are close, but they never had much in common, and they never publicized the relationship."

"Which is why," Brian murmured, "I never knew Long was Stuart's stepson. And your half brother."

"Uh-huh."

Brian took a step toward her, but only so that he could sit down on the bed. He stared at her. In spite of the sexy dress, she looked like a little girl who'd been severely scolded; he wondered if Josh was responsible for that. And he wondered why he wasn't absolutely furious with her. His principal emotion was sheer relief.

However, he wouldn't have been human if he didn't want to punish her just a bit for her tricks.

"So you pretended to be after him to make me jealous," he said. "And you asked me to teach you how to seduce a man. And you said that we could have an affair. Josh wouldn't mind; Josh wouldn't want a virgin in his bed. Was that a lie too?"

She didn't have to ask what he meant. She knew. Avoiding his intent stare she murmured, "No, it wasn't a lie. I've never had a lover."

"I'm sure it wasn't for lack of hopeful candidates," he said politely.

Serena looked at him silently.

Telling himself sternly that her guileless gray eyes weren't going to get to him *this* time, Brian went on, relentless. "All those wonderfully sweet and innocent comments of yours—planned. Cold-bloodedly. Like some general launching a campaign, you plotted to make me jealous. Is that the way it was, Serena?"

"Yes."

"Were you planning to push it all the way to the altar, or was an affair your goal?"

Serena sighed very softly, but made no attempt to defend herself or justify her actions. "The altar," she answered.

"You decided to marry me?"

"Yes."

"And just when did you come to this momentous decision?" he asked politely.

"In London. At Heathrow."

"Now for the biggie," he said dryly. "Why?"

"I fell in love with you," she answered simply.

Five

Her words caught Brian completely by surprise. He had momentarily forgotten her quiet question in the garden. But even if he had remembered, he would not have expected her to admit to love. Not now. Not after the last few minutes and his relentlessly polite grilling. It just wasn't—It didn't seem *reasonable* somehow.

"You don't expect me to believe you," he ventured to say.

"No," she said. "I've made that impossible, haven't I? I realized that tonight in the garden. More importantly, though, I realized that I'd built a wall between us higher than any you can claim."

"Walls?" He gazed at her still face. "You think I have walls? That's why you tried to trick me?"

Serena shrugged. "Does it matter now? It's over, Brian." After a moment she dropped her gaze to the jeweled watch on her wrist. "I'll call Daddy," she said, "and explain how I've put you in an impossible position. He knows me; he'll know it was my fault. He won't blame you a bit for going back to California. You don't have to let your sense of responsibility keep you here."

He waited until her gaze lifted again. "I told you. I'm in for the duration. I go back to California when you do, and not before."

Her smile was a shaky, rueful one. "I thought you'd say that. Well, I'm stuck here for a while, Brian. Daddy's orders; he needs more time. So I have to stay put to give him that time. But you don't have to worry about staying close to me. Josh is going to do so, and he's hired a private investigator to keep an eye on the hotel."

Brian kept hearing the words *I fell in love with you* over and over in his mind, but tried not to think about them. He rose to his feet slowly. "It's more serious than you told me, isn't it?"

"It wasn't . . . I didn't think it was serious when I told you. Daddy and Josh think it's serious now." She sighed, aware that her control was minimal at best. "Why don't you—talk to Josh about it, if you want to know more." She glanced at her watch again. "He's probably downstairs in the bar." With a sudden, soft laugh she added, "There's a lovely blond pianist who plays there every night."

"I'll talk to him." Remembering, abruptly, Brian added, "After I apologize to him."

Serena blinked. "For what?"

"For slugging him," he said with a growl, and stalked from the room.

Josh Long was in the dimly lit bar, as Serena had suspected he might be. The blond pianist was playing for a half-dozen or so late-night guests.

Brian spotted Josh immediately, and went directly to where the other man was seated alone in a booth. "I want to apologize," he said.

"Think nothing of it," Josh responded instantly. "Join me? I'll buy you a drink." If there was a slight swelling in his jaw, only Brian's guilty conscience could see it. Josh, at least, didn't appear to be aware of it, or in pain.

Brian slid into the booth across from the dark younger man, but said, "I'll buy. I owe you that, at least." He thought privately that he owed considerably more.

Josh smiled, but said nothing. He studiously avoided looking up at the brunette cocktail waitress while he gave his order and listened to Brian's, then he said dryly, "I've been caught in a few of Serena's plots before now. Believe me, you reacted naturally."

"Has she *always* done things like this?" Brian asked incredulously.

Josh pulled a gold cigarette case from his inside pocket, not answering until his cigarette was lighted. Then, with a chuckle, he said, "I think the first plot involved saving four homeless puppies. In fact she got a neighborhood animal shelter established—which is still operating to this day. Rena was seven at the time."

Brian thought about that. "Remarkable. But still . . . A plot like this one. You knew . . . I mean—"

"Knew she wanted to marry you?" Josh nodded. "I knew. Sorry about my part in all this, by the way, even if it was only window dressing. Serena's always been able to wrap me around her little finger, I'm afraid. There's usually no danger in that." He looked at Brian from hooded eyes. "She has an innate ability to make most people happy. Tricks and all."

Brian avoided the look, sipping his drink slowly. He couldn't fight his own curiosity, and he couldn't stop his sharp mind from working. "Control," he said suddenly. "That's it, isn't it?"

Josh followed the thought unerringly. "Control. It probably wouldn't have become so much a part of her personality, except for Mother's death."

Brian met that hooded gaze steadily. "But your mother was killed."

Nodding slowly Josh said, "Under very difficult circumstances. Serena was ten; there was no way to keep the truth from her. She learned, long before she should have, that there were cruel, malevolent people in the world. People who were willing to destroy to get what they wanted. It wasn't a—very nice lesson. It was a lesson never forgotten."

It chilled Brian to think of a ten-year-old little girl's tragically shocking realization that people could be unspeakably cruel, impersonally vicious.

Softly he said, "Ten years old. She could have withdrawn, become possessive of those she loved. She could have learned to mistrust, to be wary and frightened. It would have been completely natural, even expected."

Josh nodded. "Instead she became even more softhearted and—I think—even more innocent. She's complex, layers and layers to her, but the core, the basic core, is still vulnerable and insanely trusting."

Oddly enough, Brian found no paradox there. It

made sense to him somehow. Because it was Serena they were discussing, it made sense.

Abruptly Josh said, "She hasn't told you about her children."

It wasn't a question, but Brian answered, "No, she hasn't."

"Foster kids. All over the world. And she doesn't just give money to support them, she sends letters, presents. She visits them if she can. And she keeps up with the news, the politics, of every country where one of her kids lives. She worries about them but never talks about them. The pictures they send her are tacked up all over her bedroom at home."

"Layers," Brian murmured.

Josh watched him for a moment, then said softly, "She's honest except when it would hurt someone or when she's up to her tricks. And even when she's plotting, it tends to be evasion or implication rather than lies. The scary thing is that she's almost always right. In fact I've never known her to be wrong. Except maybe this time."

Brian didn't take the bait. He was afraid of what he'd most likely catch. Changing the subject determinedly he said, "These implied threats to Stuart, what about them?"

Accepting the change, Josh sighed. "Didn't look like much at first; Stuart's dealt with worse. But we found out a few days ago that you two were traced as far as Wichita. And Stuart's contacts in the intelligence community aren't having much luck in finding out who's behind it all. That in itself is unusual enough to put us on alert."

"If these people found Serena," Brian said slowly, "what would they do?"

"Take her, probably. Before she could get away again," Josh answered bluntly. "Hold her somewhere as a threat. Use her to force Stuart to give in. And he would, of course, if she were in danger. They know that."

"Would they hurt her?"

"If Stuart refused to give in," Josh said levelly.

Brian believed him. Still, he could hardly help but protest. "But if they kidnap Serena and force Stuart to give in to them, he'll know for certain who's behind it all! And with a serious crime like that to charge them with—"

Josh was shaking his head. "The corporate power guys behind this plot could never be traced. That would be too easy. Whoever does their dirty work will be professionals, with no connection whatsoever to the power men; and whoever makes Stuart the offer will do so in all innocence, completely ignorant of any threats or coercion."

"Then how in God's name does Stuart expect to track them down?" Brian asked violently.

Josh smiled just a little. "Sure you want to know?"

"I want to know."

"All right. First consider the entire situation. Someone—unknown—wants Stuart. And this someone is prepared to play some very dirty games to get him. Now, we both know business is sometimes dirty, but for most of us respectable businessmen it usually stops short of violence. But not these guys. Rarely do they have the best interests of the economy or our country at heart."

Josh reflected for a moment in silence, then went on. "In spite of having left the intelligence community years ago, Stuart very naturally keeps in touch. The community knows the danger of a scientist of Stuart's caliber working for the wrong people. So it's more than willing to help to avert that danger.

"Right now a number of people are trying to trace the men who were asking questions about the two of you in Wichita. The trail is a tangled one, but movements can be traced. Eventually the intelligence people will discover who these men work for. They won't have courtroom proof, you understand, but they'll be certain."

Brian did understand. "And when they're certain?"

Josh smiled faintly. "That's when the intelligence people can trace the nice, respectable, powerful men behind this whole thing. Then they'll start what the law so cruelly calls harassment. Nothing overt. Nothing illegal. Soon after that, these powerful men will begin to have problems with their businesses. Small problems. A great many small problems. Costly problems."

"Trade-offs." Brian came to the realization slowly. "The intelligence community trades off with law enforcement."

Nodding, Josh said, "It's done all the time. Very quietly. You scratch my back, and I'll scratch yours. They're masters at it. And they'll make it so quietly hot for the businessmen, they'll decide it just isn't worth it."

"How long will that take?"

"Not as long as you might think. These 'businessmen' will figure out pretty quickly what's happening. And they'll move to cut their losses."

For a while the two men were silent. Brian beckoned the waitress, and they ordered fresh drinks. He noted that the other man seemed to avoid so much as a glance at the waitress; he was mildly curious, but unwilling to ask questions. Finally, with their drinks in front of them and the waitress gone again, Brian focused on his paramount worry.

"What're the chances these men will find Serena before any moves can be made against them?"

Josh looked grim. "Their chances get better with every day that passes. All we can do is be on guard until we find out who's behind this."

"Dammit, that's— She should be somewhere safe. Protected." Brian felt violent.

"Surrounded by guards?" Josh shook his head. "In the first place Rena wouldn't stand for it; she remembers too well being guarded after Mother was killed. But, even more, it would alert the men behind this. They'd call off their dogs and our trail would end right there. Then, when the smoke cleared and Serena was no longer being guarded, they'd grab her. She'd be missing, we'd be hamstrung, and Stuart would have to give in."

Brian could see the logic; it was inescapable. But he wasn't happy about it.

Josh read his expression clearly. "It probably won't make you feel any better," he said dryly, "but Serena can take care of herself. Stuart made sure both of us could; he was very careful about that. As a result she's skilled in the martial arts. She even knows a few exotic techniques specifically designed for small ladies. I'd hate to tangle with her, and I'm a black belt."

"It makes me feel a little better," Brian confessed.

Josh finished his drink, then sent a regretful glance toward the blond pianist. "I think I'll turn in. It's been a long day. The P.I.'s already on the job; he'll keep an eye on things tonight. I gather you aren't returning to California?"

Brian shook his head. "I'm staying." They both rose to their feet, and left the bar. Brian glanced around the lobby as they passed through, but saw no one who fit his image of a private investigator.

"In the corner," Josh murmured.

Taking a surreptitious look, Brian saw the man. He was middle-aged, and ordinary in every respect, and was flirting outrageously with the waitress who had served them their drinks.

In the elevator going up, Brian said uneasily, "Are you sure he's the right man for the job? Seemed careless."

"He's fine, believe me."

Brian accepted his word, trusting that Stuart's stepson had experience in these matters.

Josh's room was a floor above Brian's, so the men said good night in the elevator. Without Josh's company Brian immediately found that thinking, however confused his thoughts, came far too easily. And as worried as he was over Serena's safety, the words *I fell in love with you* were still whirling in his mind.

He hadn't responded to those words, he remembered, except to say, "Do you expect me to believe you?"

That, more than anything else, bothered him. His emotions were impossibly tangled. And between the more intimate knowledge of her that Josh had offered and his own strong feelings,

Brian was certain that, however many layers Serena wrapped herself in, she was basically a very vulnerable woman.

A woman who could be hurt.

Thoughts of plots and tricks were forgotten. Brian remembered only a little girl weathering a tragic shock and a woman who had looked at him with quiet eyes and spoken not a single word in defense of herself.

He wasn't surprised to find himself knocking softly at her door. He heard movement, then a brief silence before the quiet clatter of the night chain, and the door opened. She had first looked through the security peephole, he realized, and he was glad she was at least that careful.

She was dressed for bed, and his breath caught in his throat at the lovely picture she made in the floor-length violet gown and negligee, her hair loose and feet bare. Then he saw her red-rimmed eyes, and his heart lurched when he realized she'd been crying.

She gestured silently for him to come in, then closed the door and followed him into the room. "Have you talked to Josh?" Her voice was soft.

Brian turned to face her. "Yes. He explained the situation."

"And?"

He understood her question. "I'm staying."

Serena drew a deep breath, then said hesitantly, "Since you're staying, maybe we . . . Well, I know you won't forgive me for the tricks, but maybe we could still be friends?"

"Just friends?"

"I—yes."

He reached to cup her cheek in his warm hand. "I don't think so, Serena." He saw and felt a slight tremor within her.

"I was afraid of that," she murmured.

Evenly he said, "I don't think it's possible for you and me to be just friends. More, or less, but never just friends."

She looked at him silently, waiting.

"We can't go back," he said, "and this seems to be a hell of a time to go forward. But I'm willing if you are."

"You're just feeling responsible for me. I don't want that, Brian!"

"I am feeling responsible," he admitted quietly. "But not because I think of you as a kid, and not because you're Stuart's daughter."

"Then why?" she whispered.

He was silent for a long moment, looking intently at her, as though he were searching for something. "I'm not quite sure," he said finally. "Maybe because you seem vulnerable in spite of your tricks. And maybe because the tricks worked." His voice was wry, the admission a reluctant one.

She returned his intent gaze uncertainly. "You mean you were—".

"Jealous?" He smiled. "Why do you think I knocked Josh down? Not out of any sense of responsibility, I can tell you that. You're of age, after all; who am I to get angry over your interest in another man? But I did get angry, Rena. I'm not entirely sure how I feel about you, but I couldn't stand the thought of your being with him."

Serena sighed shakily. "Then you think we should go on from here?"

He nodded. "I don't know where we'll end up. I can't make you any promises, Rena."

Serena didn't ask him to explain that; she merely nodded. It was enough, and more than she'd dared hope for. She had another chance with Brian, and this time she resolved to be completely herself, with no plot driving her.

Of course, that wasn't to say something wouldn't occur to her later.

The next day should have been an awkward day for them both, and would have been, except for the terrible Bishop kids. Brian had forgotten all about Serena's promise to baby-sit.

He wished she had too.

On waking, Brian discovered a message from Serena that she had elected to keep the children for the entire day, and that they would remain in the hotel or garden.

He ordered breakfast from room service to fortify himself.

He considered staying in his room for the day, but he very quickly found that he was too anxious over Serena's safety. He checked her room, and, since it was empty, he sighed and went in search of her and the Terrible Two.

Brian didn't quite know how to greet Serena. Their good nights had been constrained, and now he was feeling very guarded and uncertain. He still wasn't quite sure why he had forgiven her scheming and why he was willing—eager, even—to allow their relationship to progress.

And, since he was not a man who was often

uncertain about anything, the feeling disturbed him.

Walls. She had said he had walls, yet she hadn't defined those barriers; he had a strong feeling she could have, though.

And that bothered him too. How, he wondered, could she define what he couldn't define himself? He had told her he didn't want to get involved, she'd said. He honestly couldn't remember telling her that.

And if he *had* told her—what were his reasons? Why then, when he had expected only to escort Stuart's daughter home? Why, for that matter, tell her at all?

"Oh, the hell with it," Brian muttered, then flushed as he suddenly became aware of the startled look from the elderly lady sharing the elevator. He added a hasty, "Pardon me," and was very glad when the doors opened seconds later to reveal the lobby.

His relief was momentary, however, and very soon supplanted by annoyance.

Serena looked up from her comfortable position on a love seat to see Brian striding toward her and carrying little Mark Bishop under one arm like an unwanted feed sack. The man's handsome face spoke volumes for the fact that he was unhappy with his towheaded appendage; Mark, on the other hand, was clearly delighted by his mode of transportation.

"This little monster," Brian announced without preamble and in a tone of careful precision, "had a snare set by the elevators." Still dangling the giggling Mark, Brian produced a coiled length of twine from his pocket and held it out like an indictment. "Stretched across to trip the unwary —of which I was nearly one," he elaborated coldly.

With a wink directed at Mark's freckled, grinning face, Serena said mildly, "Well, that was clever of him, don't you think? I didn't know how to set a snare at his age."

"I should hope not!" Brian snapped. The arm curled around Mark shifted, so that the boy was dangled in front of Brian as though he were an offering for sacrifice. "He could have badly injured someone!"

Still mild, Serena said, "Oh, I don't think he would have let that happen. You wouldn't have, would you, Mark?"

" 'Course not," Mark chirped up, clearly undismayed by his present position. "I would've taken prisoners. It was a ambush," he explained loftily.

"You're standin' on my puzzle!" scolded a voice from Brian's feet.

He stepped aside hastily and dropped Mark on the love seat beside Serena as he looked down to find Lisa Bishop's angelic, China-blue eyes glaring up at him. "It shouldn't be on the floor," he told her firmly.

"Well, it is," she announced, her tone daring him to dispute the fact of the matter.

Brian, who had had little experience with children before encountering Serena, looked to her rather helplessly.

Serena smiled. "Lisa is very intelligent. She's putting together a thousand-piece puzzle. Could you do that at her age?"

Brian, estimating Lisa's age to be around six, said that he couldn't have. That he hadn't wanted to.

"Help me!" Lisa demanded imperiously.

"No." Brian sat down in a chair flanking the love seat and tried to ignore what had mysteriously become a heartrending appeal from China-blue eyes. Serena, who had an excellent idea of just how long he'd be able to withstand that appeal, snagged the twine from his fingers and began explaining the construction of a cat's cradle for Mark's enjoyment.

Moments later, her peripheral vision having recorded Brian's capitulation, she muttered, "The bigger they are, the easier they fall."

"Bite your tongue," Brian told her absently as he frowned over a baffling puzzle piece.

During the next few hours he had to bite his own tongue more than once to keep from swearing out loud. Mark was the cause, for the most part, although it soon became apparent that Lisa's innocent eyes hid the soul of a gremlin.

In spite of having two pairs of adult eyes to watch them, the children had obviously perfected the art of slipping off their respective leashes in order to get into mischief. And the ability to get into mischief seemed an inborn talent.

Lost for ten minutes, Mark was discovered building a jungle from the potted palms near the elevators, where he launched unprovoked attacks on passersby. Listening interestedly to Brian's stern reprimand, his explanation—Mark never excused himself—was that he had been experimenting in the art of guerrilla warfare.

Brian blinked.

"Intelligent, isn't he?" Serena said.

Deciding that the boy was obviously the greater troublemaker, Brian took pains to interest him in something safe, and ended up immersed in the construction of a model plane purchased in the hotel gift shop. That there were pitfalls in even that innocent pastime was proven when Mark playfully glued three ashtrays to their respective tables before Brian could catch him.

"Nail-polish remover," Serena murmured, "will dissolve the glue."

"I always knew I approved of planned parenthood," was Brian's only remark. "Now I know why."

Having a lively sense of self-preservation, Mark clearly deduced from Brian's expression that a moderation of behavior was called for, and so behaved like an angel. For a while.

Brian suspected that the whole thing was planned, for while Mark was an angel, Lisa became a gremlin.

She disappeared into the garden, where she spent the few moments before discovery trying to catch goldfish in the ornamental pool. Then she vanished into the gift shop, where she was found to be critically modeling a scanty lace teddy over her T-shirt and blue jeans. Then she somehow slipped behind the front desk and pressed what turned out to be the panic button on the main computer, sending the entire system into chaos.

Brian found himself soothing a number of upset people, spreading largess here, bribes there, and holding on to his own temper with both hands.

He then very calmly picked up a child with each

arm and disappeared with them to his room after telling Serena to wait for them in the lobby. When the three returned some time later, both Mark and Lisa were subdued and cast glances of mingled respect and resentment at Brian.

And they behaved for the remainder of the day.

Collected by their parents—who appeared to have shed ten years in a single day minus their offspring—Mark and Lisa solemnly and without prompting thanked Serena and Brian, and both hugged Serena affectionately.

Mark then offered a manly handshake to Brian, and Lisa hugged him, somewhat to his surprise. He was even more surprised to discover himself returning the hug with an abrupt surge of affection.

"You," Serena told him thoughtfully when the Bishops had departed, "would make a very good father." Then she flushed suddenly and avoided his eyes.

"I've never thought much about it," he said gently.

"I know."

He looked at her. "How do you know?"

After a moment she sighed and returned his gaze. "I know," she said, "because it makes sense. I'll bet you knew when you were in high school that you wanted to build your own company. Right?" She waited for his nod. "And since that time, you've worked toward that end. You started the firm, built it up, made it a success. Brian, you haven't had time for thinking of anything but the company in years. Except," she added dryly, "for an occasional 'relationship.' And since you were in a rut, you probably didn't *think* about the relationships."

"What do you mean by *rut*?" he asked, astonished.

"Slip of the tongue."

"The hell it was. It was deliberate. Now explain it."

Serena was smiling, an elusive emotion that might have been humor dancing in her eyes. "All right," she said, continuing with firm deliberation. "You, Brian, are in a rut. The chains of habit bind you. I'll bet you haven't taken an unplanned step since high school—and possibly not since elementary school."

Brian knew intellectually that she had glibly translated a disciplined nature into what sounded uncomfortably like a boring one; he reacted emotionally. "That's—nonsense," he said, having obviously changed his mind and substituted "nonsense" for a less polite word.

"Is it?" Serena rose from the edge of the ornamental pool where they'd been sitting since the Bishops had reclaimed their offspring, and looked down at him, still smiling. In a tone that could not *quite* be called sympathetic, she said, "According to all the statistics, a single man in his mid-thirties is generally single out of sheer habit. Usually because he concentrated on building a career in his twenties. So he gets in a rut. Begins to believe he has this strong reason for staying single—when all the time it's just a habit. And habits are terribly hard to break, you know."

Brian rose slowly to his feet and stared at her. "I think I'm getting the hang of this," he said, as though to a third person. Then, to Serena, he said pleasantly, "You're trying to provoke me."

Serena glanced idly toward the setting sun, then

back at him. "Am I? Why, Brian, I'm just making an observation."

"You're trying to provoke me," he repeated firmly. He was, at that moment, very sure that he was right. "You think I'm going to—It's reverse psychology. You tell me I'm in a rut, so I immediately 'break out' of that rut by deciding to do something . . . reckless."

"That makes me sound very cunning," she commented, thoughtful.

"You are," he told her. "And it won't work."

Serena smiled. "What're we going to do about dinner?"

He blinked. "What do you want to do?"

"Eat."

From his momentary position of certainty, Brian felt himself again falling into bewilderment. He had so completely accepted the reality of Serena's plotting that he had found himself searching for motives behind every utterance. But was there motive behind every word she spoke? Could she possibly be that devious? Or was he imagining things?

"And then?" he asked guardedly.

"We could play poker," she suggested gently, then turned and headed for the hotel.

Six

During the next two days Brian couldn't decide if Serena had indeed abandoned her plotting or if she was playing a wonderful game of poker.

She never again referred to his "rut" or to the habits of bachelors. Nor did she refer to her earlier decision to get him to the altar. But she did continue to go to dinner wearing evening gowns that turned heads and stopped conversations in mid-sentence.

There was, however, a change in her behavior.

From their first meeting, Serena had proven herself to be a woman who liked to touch. It was, he had thought then, part of her charm. She would slide her hand beneath his arm as they walked or touch his hand when they talked. Her gestures had seemed innocent, confiding.

He would have been suspicious of such gestures now, had they been made. But they were not. Without being obvious about it, Serena refrained from touching him.

And she had stopped flirting. No more provocative questions or remarks. No more slow Mona Lisa smiles. No more enigmatic glances from smoky gray eyes. She was casual and friendly, but not intimate. She made him laugh with comical stories of some of her past plots; she talked quietly, after a bald question from him, about her foster children. They played cards, alone and with Josh, who seemed secretly amused about something. They shared every meal, walked in the garden, played tennis and golf, went horseback riding, and talked.

Brian found himself watching her warily at first, then with increasing intentness. He made a few provocative remarks of his own, and Serena either ignored them, missed them—impossible, he knew—or else smoothly changed the subject.

He wondered if Serena was too conscious of her previous scheme's failure to be able to let their relationship progress naturally. He wondered if this was a new plot. If so, he was wryly amused to realize that it was working.

Thinking about it, he wasn't surprised. Serena had first been a responsibility in his eyes. Amusing, troublesome, yet still a responsibility. Later, almost in the blink of an eye, she had shown herself to be a fascinating, desirable woman, igniting his senses and confusing all rational thought. Then she had confessed her plotting with childlike simplicity and no excuses.

From child to woman to child—and now back to woman. A friendly, cheerful woman who needed to give no sultry glances or enigmatic smiles to remind a man she was all female. A lady who wore stunning evening gowns with the same simple grace with which she wore jeans or slacks, who now offered no confiding touches or provocative words, and yet somehow made a man stingingly aware of her every casual gesture.

She was damnably intriguing.

Brian found that he could actually *feel* his heart beating in her presence, a strong and uneven rhythm. He missed her casual touches, finding excuses himself to make contact with her. He felt a growing tension that was as emotional as it was physical, disturbing his sleep and making him uncharacteristically restless.

On the third night after her confession, he demanded of Josh, "What in hell is she up to?" He didn't have to elaborate.

"I don't know," Josh told him, obviously amused. They were all three playing cards in the quiet lounge off the lobby, with drinks and snacks nearby, and Serena had excused herself briefly. "I suppose," Josh said judiciously, "she's plotting. But I'm damned if I'm sure. Even after knowing her all her life, I have an uncomfortable feeling Rena could surprise me once a day if she wanted to. You have to admit that she isn't dull."

The only answer to that vast understatement seemed to be a drink, so Brian took a gulp of his. It didn't help. He hadn't really expected it to.

Serena came back into the room just as her half brother looked at his watch and stacked his cards neatly. "Deal me out," he told them as he stood up. "I have a date."

"The pianist?" Serena murmured.

"As a matter of fact, yes."

In an idle tone, Serena said, "You know, it's common practice for women to change their hair color. And when they do, it's usually from brunette to blond. But I don't suppose that matters, does it, Josh?"

Her half brother stared down at her for a moment, then said in a peculiar tone to Brian, "I told you she could still surprise me." Without another word he left the room.

"I wonder if he'll break the date," Serena mused.

Brian stared at her. "What was that all about?"

"His fixation."

"Come again?"

Shuffling cards expertly, Serena laughed softly. "Hadn't you noticed? It isn't blondes Josh is obsessed with, it's brunettes. And he thought I didn't know." She shook her head in a gentle reproof of her absent kin.

"Know *what*?" Brian asked, still confused.

"Well, Josh is one of those rare people who has always *known* himself. I mean, he always understands why he likes or dislikes something. He doesn't have to ponder it; he just knows. I think in some ways he's a bit psychic, about himself, anyway. And being a healthy, self-preserving male, he wants complete control of his life." She reflected, almost in surprise. "We're alike in that way."

"The point being?"

"The point being that he *knows* when he falls in love, it'll be with a brunette, and he'll fall hard," she added with certainty.

"How could he possibly know he'll fall in love with a brunette?" Brian asked in bewilderment.

"He just does. He's never dated a brunette in his life, and a few truly gorgeous ones have tried to get his attention, I can tell you. But Josh—like you—avoids lengthy relationships. You pointed out once yourself that he's—um—uncomfortably close to being a rake. I don't think it's habit with him; it's the need to keep control of his life."

"Ever thought of hanging out a shingle?"

Serena smiled. "Oh, I'm no armchair psychologist. But I know Josh. His fear is based on the certainty that a brunette will be his downfall. And I only hope I'm around to see it, because it'll be something to watch. Josh doesn't rattle easily, but I'll bet some dark-haired beauty will knock him flat on his back."

After a long moment, Brian said slowly, "You don't like to lose control either. That night in the garden you said, 'I won't lose control of this.' " He hadn't known quite how to phrase the question, and thought she would probably change the subject anyway. But Serena fooled him.

She met his gaze squarely. "But I'd already lost control," she confessed. "I found out what Josh will find out one day. You can't control love. It isn't made that way. It just happens, like an act of nature."

He felt he had to say something, but didn't know what it was.

Shaking her head, she said softly, "I thought I could control you and me, thought I could make you love me. I was wrong. You were right; there's too much between us. Or not enough."

Brian stared at her, his throat aching. Clearing it strongly, he said, "Nobility, Serena?"

Unoffended, she thought about that. "No, I don't think so. Odd as it sounds, I'm a realist. If something doesn't work, then it doesn't work. For whatever reasons, you don't want a commitment. I do."

"You agreed we should let our relationship progress," he reminded her, conscious of the tightness in his voice.

She nodded. "I know. But it hasn't."

"And you don't think it will? You're very calm about it." He wondered how she could be, if indeed she believed herself to be in love with him. She looked away from his stare, but not before he caught a glimpse of sudden pain in her eyes. What bothered him the most was that she *had* looked away; for the first time she was hiding her vulnerability from him.

"What do you want me to say, Brian? That I'm heartbroken? We both know hearts don't break. They just hurt. But we don't die from the pain, even though we sometimes think we will. Time heals—a cliché, but only because everyone knows it's true. Well, I'm hurting, if you want to know."

It wasn't an accusation, but Brian felt the sting of his own conscience. That . . . and something else, a new pain he couldn't define.

She smiled at him, her gray eyes tranquil again. "It isn't your fault you can't love me, Brian. I'd be hell for you anyway. I'd disrupt your orderly life."

With a faint sense of surprise, he heard his taut voice. "You give up too easily."

"Then what should I do, Brian?" Her voice was quiet. "Play Let's Pretend? Let's pretend I never plotted in the first place. Let's pretend you'll never feel trapped. Let's pretend we'll have an affair and not hurt when it's over. Let's pretend I don't need a promise you can't give."

His throat was aching again. "Rena—"

"I suppose I'm an anachronism. Out of step. I suppose I should say, 'Oh, what the hell, passion might become love.' But I can't say that. And you wouldn't believe me if I did. But if you want to pretend, Brian, I won't say no."

She looked down at the cards still in her hand. Softly she added, "I couldn't say no to anything you asked of me. Don't you know that?"

Brian couldn't take his eyes off her still, averted face. "Is that why you've been acting as if I never held you in my arms?" he asked huskily.

She nodded almost imperceptibly. "I can't control this, remember? You wouldn't have to ask, wouldn't even have to touch me. Your room or mine, it wouldn't matter, not tonight. But in the morning . . . I'd know there'd be an ending. And you'd feel guilty, because you'd know I needed more than one night, more than an affair."

Her soft, honest words stole his breath away, and Brian could feel his heart pounding. And he hurt, because a stubborn part of him was still unwilling to consider commitment. "I don't want to hurt you," he said.

Serena looked at him finally, her eyes darkening. "And I don't want to be hurt. But I don't want to live this way anymore—in limbo. I can't stand the sleepless nights, and being afraid to touch you." She drew an unsteady breath. "Let's pretend, Brian. Let's make believe it won't matter in the morning, or next week."

Brian had to grip the arms of his chair tightly to prevent himself from jumping up and taking her in his arms. "How long could we make believe, Rena?" he asked harshly. "How long before you'd hate me for what I'd done to you?"

"I wouldn't hate you," she told him quietly. "I don't even think I'd hate myself. I'm a grown woman, Brian; I know what I'm saying. I want you. And I'm asking you to let me make that decision."

He knew the struggle within him was obvious, knew she saw what it cost him to refuse. "No," he said, finally, hoarsely. "No, Rena, I can't let you do that." Stiffly, feeling his entire body ache, he rose from his chair and left the room.

When Josh stepped into the lounge some three hours later, he found Serena seated alone. The clutter they had left earlier was gone. There was a soft drink beside her, and she was absently dealing crooked poker hands to imaginary players.

"Where's Brian?" Josh asked, sinking down in a chair.

"In his room, I think." She looked at him. "Was the blonde really a blonde?"

"I didn't ask," he retorted.

Serena smiled, gathered up her cards, and went about methodically stacking the deck for another crooked deal. He watched her, interested, and waited until she'd dealt the cards before commenting critically, "A nine doesn't belong in a royal flush; you're slipping."

She ignored the information. "Josh, a hypothetical situation."

Josh, who knew very well that stating a hypothetical situation was something like announcing that one had a "friend" with a problem, nodded blandly. "I'm listening."

She appeared to gather her thoughts, and then spoke slowly. "You have very honestly made it plain to someone that he or she has the power to hurt you. If this person takes a certain action, you're going to be hurt eventually. The action itself won't hurt you, but the ramifications will. Both of you *want* the action to take place, but he—this other person—refuses because he *knows* you'll be hurt."

Josh, perfectly aware of what they were talking about, nodded. "I see. And so?"

Serena gave him a frustrated look. "Don't be dense."

He smiled. "All right, I won't be. You're saying that Brian has refused to—uh—advance your relationship physically because he knows that, for you, it's forever, while for him it isn't."

She winced, but nodded.

"This is a hell of a conversation to be having with my sister," Josh said parenthetically.

"We've always been able to talk about things that matter to us," she reminded him. "So talk. Tell me what to do."

Josh waited, and, as he'd expected, Serena began shaping the situation verbally so that she could see it clearly.

"By being honest, I've painted both of us into a corner. He knows I love him; he knows how I feel about having an affair. I've set it up wonderfully," she said bitterly, "so that he'll feel hellishly guilty for taking advantage of this—this physical chemistry between us. Dammit, Josh, I don't *want* him to feel guilty! How can I convince him that I'll feel cheated for the rest of my life unless I—unless we—Oh, *hell!*"

After a moment Josh said gently, "Have you told him that?"

"That I'd feel cheated? No, not in those words. Would you feel guilty in the same situation?"

He nodded immediately. "Guilty. Responsible."

"Trapped," she added with a bitter tone. Then, defiantly, she went on. "Why should he feel guilty just because I have this masochistic desire to be hurt?"

Quietly Josh answered. "Because he'll be the one holding the lash."

Her defiance melted away. She shook her head in a gesture of defeat. "Yes. Yes, I know that. I've really messed things up, haven't I?"

"You were honest; you couldn't be anything else once you'd stopped plotting."

Serena sighed. "I suppose."

She gathered the cards back up, shuffling them absently. "I just don't know what to do about it," she murmured. "Unless I could get him drunk and take advantage of him. He could hardly blame himself then, could he?"

Dryly Josh said, "Contrary to what you obviously believe, liquor is not an aphrodisiac. In fact, it tends to have somewhat of a dampening effect."

"Oh." She looked at him, started to say something, then fell silent for a long moment. Abstractedly she said, "I'm surprised he hasn't come looking for me. He's never left me completely alone since he found out about Daddy's troubles, unless I was safely locked in my room."

Josh hesitated, then said, "Well, he didn't leave you completely alone this time. He stopped in the lobby and ordered the P.I. to keep an eye on you."

She laughed a little, then rose to her feet and laid the cards aside. "I think I'll turn in. Why don't you call Brian and tell him you saw me safely to my room?"

"Not unless I do," Josh told her firmly, rising also.

"Ummm." She looked at him thoughtfully. "Meet me by the elevators, then, okay? I want to speak to the desk clerk before I go up."

Josh felt honor-bound to ask what she was up to *now*, but decided not to. He had a strong feeling that what he didn't know this time wouldn't disturb his sleep. He didn't even want to speculate about it.

A brother was better off not knowing details.

Dawn's light was filtering through the drapes when Brian woke with a start. He'd lain awake most of the night, restless and troubled, and wasn't really surprised that the dream that had awakened him had been decidedly erotic. Soft hands touching him, and the elusive scent of a familiar perfume . . .

Then, as Brian got both eyes open and functioning, his breath caught in his throat.

"You left the night chain off," Serena said huskily. "I thought you probably would."

She was there in reality, in his bed. His senses ignited when he realized that only the blankets covered her and only a pocket of warm air separated them. She was on one elbow, watching him, the blankets gathered to barely cover her breasts.

Beautiful.

"Serena—" he choked out, fighting the urges she had unleashed with her very simple and straightforward action.

Silently she reached out to touch his chest, her fingers exploring the mat of dark gold hair and the tensing muscles beneath.

He trapped her hand against him, forcing out words. "No, Serena, for God's sake! I told you I wouldn't let you—"

She didn't bother to argue. Instead she moved closer to him, abandoning her loose hold on the blankets, her lips feathering softly along his jaw. Brian felt the press of her breast against his arm, and what sanity he could still claim spun off into oblivion.

Groaning, he surrounded her with his arms, pulling her even closer, feeling an electric shock as he pressed her slender body to his. His fingers tangled in her thick, silky hair, and his lips found hers in urgent demand as he rolled until she lay half under him. Serena's arms wound up around his neck and her mouth responded instantly, opening to him, inviting his possession.

He seemed to kiss her forever, as if the touch of her lips satisfied a desperate craving, one hand still tangled in her hair and the other beneath her back. But it wasn't enough for either of them, and his mouth moved with the same urgent need to plunder the soft skin at her neck.

Serena flung her head back, gasping because she couldn't breathe, trembling because she couldn't move and had to somehow. Her hands gripped his shoulders, then slid downward to mold firm, rippling muscles and explore a straight spine. He was warm and hard and strong, and a liquid heat swirled within her. In a flashing instant the seducer had become the seduced. A frantic necessity filled her aching body as a soft moan tore from her throat.

She moved beneath him, her spine arching upward, her breasts brushing against the thick hair on his chest. Instantly she felt as though an electric current had raced from him to her, and her breasts were suddenly heavy, stinging.

He shuddered at her touch, muscles clenching, his fingers beneath her pressing her soft flesh, and a low sound escaped him. Compulsively she arched against him again, shuddering as he did, her fingers digging into his back.

Serena felt like a puppet, her strings pulled by mindless desire. Never in her life had she so lost control of herself. And she felt the shock of realizing her own abandonment was a release, a heady, dizzying freedom. No thoughts of the future were allowed to intrude; there was only now and this glorious, bold fearlessness.

She had taken the right step. Nothing that felt like this could ever be wrong.

"Dear heaven, Rena . . ." His voice was thick, impeded, his chest moving strongly with every harsh breath. His lips burned a trail down between her breasts and both hands moved to surround the full, aching weight of them. Then his mouth captured a hard, aching nipple, and Serena arched into him again with a broken, breathless cry.

What she felt then, a terrible, violent need to have him closer than he could ever be, made her understand for the first time how loving could be madness. She was helpless against it, utterly unable to withstand the demands of her body for his.

If she had known that certain death would follow his possession, she would not have been able to turn away from him, would have gone happily to her end . . .

Brian's hand was sliding over her flesh, tracing her narrow rib cage and tiny waist, smoothing the curve of her hip. She locked her fingers in his hair and held him, eyes closed, all her consciousness focused on his hand, on his mouth tugging at her breast, his hungry, swirling tongue.

She could feel him tremble against her, feel the urgency of his body as he moved. His hand roamed over her thigh, seeking, and she jerked convulsively with a smothered moan when he found her warmth. Instantly the ache in her grew, hollow and hurting almost unbearably, the boundaries of it expanding until she felt nothing but emptiness and desperate need. A need for something she could not even put into words.

"Brian . . ." Her voice was a thread of sound, her plea a mindless, wordless one.

"You're so beautiful," he muttered hoarsely, his

head lifting and green eyes glowing with incandescent desire. "So warm . . ." His fingers explored gently, stroking, and she bit her lip with a gasp at the pleasure his touch evoked. Her hands moved to his shoulders and gripped hard.

She cradled him instinctively when he moved over her, her eyes fixed on his taut face, her breath coming quickly. She could feel another seeking touch, and then he was kissing her, deep, drugging kisses that stole what little breath she had. She tried to draw him closer, blind instinct guiding her, but Brian resisted.

"I'll hurt you." He groaned, his eyes glazed, voice strained. "I don't want to hurt you." Then he groaned again, and his eyes closed briefly in anguish. "Damn, what am I saying? This is only the beginning of the hurt. . . ."

Words, she somehow knew, would never reassure him. She arched upward, her breasts brushing against him, lips seeking the tense angle of his jaw. Her hands caressed the clenched muscles of his back, her arms drawing him insistently closer. She moved against him, and he shuddered.

"Rena—"

She could feel his need, feel his body demanding hers, and her own need made her ruthless. Now was all that mattered, and she didn't have to pretend. She touched him, stroked his rigid shoulders, her limbs entwining with his, until he groaned, defeated.

He moved suddenly, powerfully, and the pain caught her by surprise. Her eyes widened, and she cried out at the shock. But even as anxiety knifed through the glaze of passion in his eyes, she had forgotten the pain. Wonderingly she absorbed the alien fullness, the incredible closeness. A primitive possessiveness almost overwhelmed her, and her arms tightened around him.

Hers. He had made himself hers.

"Rena?" It was a breath of sound, concerned, unsteady.

In answer her body surged upward, claiming him as he had claimed her, and Brian groaned again. He moved in a steady rhythm, taking care, she realized, not to hurt her again. But Serena's body demanded as his did, and neither could control the unleashing of their ravenous need. Her every movement against him, every touch, fueled the fire until only the drive for release controlled them.

Serena felt a new, impossibly powerful tension invade her body, filling her throat. She couldn't breathe, couldn't move, and she was hurting again with a taut inner ache. She thought she'd go mad if the tension didn't ease, the ache didn't stop. She wanted to move frantically, to reach for something beyond reach, to hold tight to some anchor in the violence of her own feelings.

But there was nothing to hold to. . . .

Then, suddenly, the tension splintered and the ache swelled with a surging power, gripping her body in wild rapture. She felt she had flown without wings, breathed without air, captured a unicorn. And she had never felt closer to another human being. She felt as well as heard Brian's hoarse cry, and she cradled him tenderly as they both found a joyous peace.

His body lay heavily on hers, trembling, his

breathing harsh. He lifted his head at last, gazing at her with eyes that were still hot, eyes flickering in surprise. Serena felt a stirring within her, a renewal of passion, and instinctively held him with supple inner muscles. Brian made a soft sound deep in his chest, and bent his head to kiss her, gently at first and then with building need.

His hands caressed slowly, as though he were learning her all over again. His mouth touched and tasted. He held himself still, his restraint evoking a deep and welling passion needing nothing but their closeness to sustain it.

Their gazes locked together, dark green and smoky gray, in a communication as intimate as that of their bodies. Then suddenly Brian buried his face in her neck with a hoarse sound, and Serena held him hard, a whimper escaping her lips.

Serena felt bereft when he left her, but she was only alone for an instant. He was still touching her, stroking her body gently, and the aloneness was a fleeting thing. With a fluid motion he slipped from the bed, lifting her into his arms, kissing her. The room was dim, the heavy drapes permitting only faint light to enter, but she could see the tenderness of his expression, and gloried in it.

Moments later they were in the shower, still without lights, still curiously silent. It was a new intimacy, wordless, a rediscovery of each other's bodies slippery with soap, and kisses in the steamy heat. There was soft laughter, then the rough caress of towels as they dried each other before Brian carried her again to the bed.

He left her briefly to go to the door. A soft click told her that he had notified the world not to disturb them, and then he returned. Serena went into his arms, her body languid and warm. She rested her cheek on his hair-roughened chest, smiling as his hands stroked her back, listening to the steady beat of his heart.

Content, she slept.

The peal of the telephone was a rude intrusion on Serena's peaceful dreams, and she reached instantly to stop its demand. In her first waking moment she knew instantly where she was and whom she was with, and she turned her head to gaze dreamily at Brian's sleeping face. He was on his stomach, one arm holding her waist possessively, and she smiled as she brought the receiver to her ear.

"Hello?"

There was a moment of silence and then a dry male voice. "Well, I guessed as much."

"Morning, Josh," she murmured.

"It's almost afternoon," he told her politely.

"Is it? That's nice."

Josh laughed. "All right, I won't disturb you. Just take care you two don't starve to death, okay?"

Serena instantly felt a pang of hunger, and wondered if she would ever conquer her appetite. "We won't," she told her brother.

"I'll see you . . . when I see you."

"Bye, Josh." Serena reached to cut off the sound of his laughter, then punched for room service.

Hearing a response she said firmly, "Food. And champagne. For two."

The voice was a bit bewildered, but game. "Yes, miss. That is to Mr. Ashford's—?"

"Certainly to Mr. Ashford's room," Serena responded with hauteur.

The voice recovered its own poise. "Of course. The menu. That is, we offer an excellent brunch."

"Fine," Serena said, amiable now. "How long?"

"Three quarters of an hour, miss."

"Fine," she repeated, and cradled the receiver gently. She turned her head to watch as Brian's eyes slowly opened.

His gaze, focusing on her face, was bemused at first. Then the green eyes darkened and the arm around her waist drew her even closer. "How can I want you again when I'm barely awake?" he asked huskily.

"I don't know, but I'm glad." She turned in his arms, her own going around his neck. Her lips lifted to his, responding instantly.

"We have to talk," he murmured against her warm flesh.

She trailed a languid hand up his back, feeling a dizzying sense of power when he shuddered at her touch. "Later," she said hoarsely, probing ribs covered with hard flesh, tugging at the soft hair on his chest.

"Later. Too late. Damn you, Rena." But it was a thick caress rather than a curse, and his touch was possessive and tender, his kiss urgent.

The waiter was forced to cool his heels for some minutes after he knocked. When Brian answered the door wearing a robe, signed for the meal, and took charge of the cart himself, the waiter didn't even think of offering to open the champagne. He'd heard a giggle and a muffled curse, and knew a busy man when he saw one.

Brian rolled the cart into the room and went to open the drapes, wincing at the bright light that immediately assaulted him. When his eyes were finally adjusted to it, he turned to gaze at the lady sitting up in his bed. It took about two seconds for him to realize their food would grow cold as long as Serena remained uncovered.

He glanced around to spot what she'd worn to his room hours before, finding a scrap of lace and silk that wouldn't have offered cover for an open-minded midget. He lifted the creation, subjected it to a pained stare, then looked at her.

"You could have been awake," she said in explanation.

"So you came loaded for bear?"

"Something like that." She smiled at him.

Brian sighed, dropped the confection onto a chair, and went to unearth one of his shirts, which he tossed at her. "Put that on before I let a perfectly good meal go to waste."

Serena slipped into the shirt, then hesitated playfully before drawing it closed. "Maybe—"

"Serena."

Meekly she buttoned the shirt. But her eyes danced.

"Wanton!" he said accusingly.

"Wantin' is right," she murmured.

Brian refused to take notice of puns. He took notice of the cart instead. "Champagne," he said, startled. "Good Lord, it's our first meal of the day!"

"Champagne isn't for a time, it's for a state of mind. I was starving and happy. So, food and champagne."

Brian seemed about to say something, then shook his head and began working on the cork while Serena slid to the edge of the bed and uncovered the dishes.

Their glasses clinked together in a silent toast, and they ate while sprawled casually on the bed. Serena, as usual, ate enough for two all by herself.

"Feeding you," Brian said, "would break the budget of a small nation."

Some time later, after the dishes had been piled on the cart, he said finally, reluctantly, "It didn't change anything, Rena."

Seven

Brian braced himself for her reaction. He had expected—what had he expected? Pain? Tears? Recriminations? However, again Serena fooled him.

"I know, Brian." Her voice was gentle as always, her smile tranquil. Curled on his bed wearing only his shirt and holding a champagne glass, she was so lovely, it hurt him just to look at her.

Brian took a deep breath. "Rena, I won't make a promise I might not be able to keep."

"I don't expect you to."

He fumbled for the words to make her understand, wondering if he wanted that understanding for her sake or for his. "I don't—dammit, I didn't want to hurt you! Don't you understand that it'll be worse now?"

"Because I could forget a first love, but never a first lover?" She shook her head slightly. "No, Brian. It would have been worse if I hadn't come to you. Don't *you* understand? I would have felt cheated for the rest of my life." She hesitated, then added very softly, "There never would have been another lover, you see. Because there'll never be another love."

He groaned. "Dammit, Rena."

"Yes, I know." Her lips twisted. "That wasn't fair. I suppose I have to be so honest to atone for the tricks. But this isn't a trick, Brian. And after this we won't talk about it. When you want out, I'll know it. I won't try to hold you. It was *my* decision to take what I could. You aren't responsible for that, any more than you're responsible for my falling in love with you."

"If you're telling me not to feel guilty," he said roughly, "forget it."

Quietly, firmly, she said, "I'm telling you that I hope you'll enjoy this affair of ours every bit as much as I will. I'm not deceiving myself, and I'm not pretending—I promise you that. And I won't have any regrets when it's over."

Brian wanted to believe her. He didn't have to look too deeply into his soul to know that he couldn't have left her right now no matter what her response might have been. He had never felt as he had with Serena in his arms, never known that depth of emotion; his desire for her was stronger than it had ever been . . . and impossible to fight.

But he knew from experience that desire waned, and that was what troubled him, because she seemed certain her love would not.

"Brian." She set both their glasses aside, and went into his willing arms. "Just accept that it's a woman's prerogative to change her mind, all right?"

"I don't seem to have much choice," he murmured.

"No." She smiled at him. "You don't. I took the choice out of your hands. And now, do we really have to keep talking? Seems like an awful waste of time to me."

Brian couldn't have agreed more.

Brian stopped thinking of the future and endings and pain. He wasn't accustomed to being an ostrich, to burying his head in the sand, but he knew only too well that if he faced the reality of his relationship with Serena, it would be the beginning of the end.

And he didn't want that.

He felt a curious compulsion to grab what he could, to hold as much of Serena as he possibly could. It was an emotion he'd never felt before, and he ascribed it to his certainty that their only future was now.

He also discovered, rather to his surprise, that his fascination with Serena the woman continued, even grew stronger. The troublesome "child" he had escorted for four weeks seemed to have grown up. Yet she was still a woman who cared about people, and because she cared, she embraced their troubles.

Brian realized over the next few days that the entire hotel staff was known to her by name, from the manager right on down to the maids and maintenance people.

He had to make a few phone calls one morning to check on his company, and when those were completed, he went to the door to find out if Serena had finished changing. Her things remained in her own room, even though every night was spent in his.

He opened the door and poked his head out, surprised to see a maid coming out of Serena's room. Serena, dressed in a long terry-cloth robe, stepped out into the hall with her, and they stood talking quietly for a moment.

Watching silently Brian realized that the maid had been crying; she still dabbed at her eyes with a crumpled handkerchief. Serena pressed something into the woman's free hand with a firm gesture.

Curious, Brian left his room and headed for hers. Seeing him coming toward them the maid broke off in the middle of an impassioned jumble of words to Serena, sent him an embarrassed look, and scurried down the hall.

Serena stood on tiptoe to kiss Brian's chin when he reached her. "I'm sorry. Have you been waiting long?"

"No, I just finished the calls." He followed her into her room, enjoying as always the movements of her slender, graceful body. "What was that all about?" he asked.

Serena was stretched across the neatly made bed, scrabbling through a huge purse on the floor; she always carried it with her while traveling, but left it in her room otherwise. "What? Oh, Peggy has a problem. Did I—? No, here it is." She sat upright holding a small black address book in her hands, and began searching through it.

Tearing his gaze from the length of golden legs her movements had bared, Brian cleared his throat strongly and leaned against the low dresser. He wondered how long it would take for him to get over this strange inability to think straight in her presence. "The maid has a problem?"

"Uh-huh," Serena responded absently. "Oh, here it is." She reached for the phone. "This'll just take a minute, darling, then I'll—Hello, Matt?"

Brian felt his throat tighten as he reflected that she never used an endearment unless her mind was on something else. Consciously Serena never stooped to even the mildest emotional blackmail. Never by word, look, or gesture did she indicate possessiveness toward him.

He forced the thoughts from his mind and listened to her end of the conversation.

"Am I what? Well, I'm sorry I woke you; I keep forgetting the time zones. Of course it's important! Matt, stop yelling. You'll wake Diane. Oh, is she? Tell her I'm sorry. All right. All *right*! Well, I have a case for you. The little boy's name is Scotty Jenkins. Denver. I've given your name to his mother; she'll alert the hospital so they'll have the records ready for you. No, Matt, it's just that the bills are breaking her. No, I have a feeling the attending doctor is a little too eager to schedule surgery. Probably—eventually—but it may not be necessary just yet. The foundation can handle it. Right. Well, you did such a good job on—"

Serena's eyes focused on Brian and flickered slightly; she didn't complete the sentence.

"Will you, Matt? Thank you. Yes. And I'm sorry for waking you, really. Okay. 'Bye."

She put the receiver in its cradle and rose to her feet, smiling at Brian. "Are we still going riding? I know I packed boots—"

As she passed him to go to the closet, Brian caught her hands and stopped her. "What's wrong with the little boy?" he asked quietly.

Standing between his knees, Serena linked her hands together behind his neck. "A heart defect, poor kid," she answered readily. "Peggy's nearly frantic about him. I noticed she was worried about something, so when I saw her in the hall I asked her to come in. She needed to talk. Anyway, I happen to know of a foundation that takes care of hospital and surgical bills for kids with medical problems. Matt's a cardiac specialist; he's on the board," she finished.

Brian searched her face intently. "And who was it he did such a good job on?"

"Lots of people," she said evasively.

He had never thought of himself as an overly perceptive man, but Brian had discovered that faculty sharpened in the last weeks—and particularly in the last days. "Who, Serena?"

She stared at him for a moment, then sighed. "Me."

"You?" He felt shaken, and must have looked it.

"It was a long time ago, Brian. I was a child. It's not uncommon. I was born with a minor heart defect, which was corrected by surgery. And that's all." Her voice was matter-of-fact.

"You don't have a scar," he stated.

"Oddly enough, any scars I get fade away after a while. It's a good thing, too, because otherwise I'd look like a road map. I was a tomboy—always falling out of trees and coming home bruised."

The hands at her waist drew her suddenly closer, and Brian rested his forehead against hers. He felt cold. "There isn't any danger now?"

"None at all," she said cheerfully. "I have a perfectly normal heart." She kissed him; only when they were alone together was she demonstrative. "Now, are we going riding?"

"Maybe we—"

Serena stopped him with another kiss. "That's why I hadn't told you," she said softly. "Brian, I'm fine. Ask Josh. Or call Daddy. Look, didn't I beat you at tennis yesterday?"

He smiled slowly. "Your backhand beat me."

"Well, then."

Brian hugged her hard. He still felt shaken, almost sick, as though someone had kicked him in the stomach. And his compulsion to hold her now made it nearly impossible to release her and smile as if he were reassured. "All right. We'll go riding this afternoon. I'll call the desk and arrange for the horses."

"And I'll get dressed." She grinned at him and headed for the closet while he sat on the bed and made the call.

She went into the bathroom to dress, and it was, Brian realized, yet another subtle indication that Serena would not attempt to tie him to her. As familiar as he was with her body now, and even though she was never shy with him, Serena was also never casual.

If she undressed in front of him, it was because he started things—and she always responded instantly to whatever he initiated. In bed with him, she abandoned herself, always warmly responsive and eager, and only there would she allow herself to be the first to touch, the first to kiss. If he touched her in public, she responded; the very rare touches of her own were made only when something had distracted her.

In effect, she claimed none of a lover's rights, except when she lay in his arms.

Brian wanted to tell her, strongly, that those rights were hers. That it was her right to touch him on impulse, no matter where they were or who was watching. *"Treat me like your lover!"* he wanted to say. *"Share my room as well as my bed. Don't leave me to dress, as if even that small part of our lives is separate. Let me brush your lovely hair for you, fasten your dress. Let me watch while your tilt your head in that curiously feminine way while you put on earrings. Let me share all the casual, unguarded gestures of lovers. . . ."*

He couldn't tell her. He had denied any future for them; she had accepted that. *He* had no right to demand.

Brian heard Serena humming in the bathroom; he knew she would be completely ready when she came out. Dressed, hair arranged in whatever style she'd chosen, light makeup and jewelry in place.

She was a woman who would notice the distress of a maid, care enough to find the source of that distress, and offer compassionate help. A woman sensitive enough to see the fine distinction between an affair with a future, and one with none. And to act accordingly.

No matter what it might cost her.

Brian knew now that Serena would never again allow him to see any pain he would cause her. She had seen his pain that first morning, and she possessed the special quality of wanting to protect others from hurt whenever she could.

She didn't speak of the future, she imposed no emotional demands, and on the rare occasion that she spoke of the pleasure they found together, the word she used was a cheerful *chemistry*.

She had not spoken of love since that first morning.

When they were together, when he could look at her lovely, tranquil face or hold her in his arms, Brian forgot his own emotions. It was during the moments he spent alone, that he felt tense and unsure, that his mind was groping toward something it couldn't see, couldn't recognize.

"You're such a patient man," Serena told him readily. "Are you starving? I am."

"What else is new?" Brian said, his voice dry as he rose to his feet.

Refusing to be offended by this reference to her remarkable appetite, she preceded him to the door. She was wearing jeans that could have doubled as her skin, and a filmy silk blouse the exact shade of her gray eyes. Her hair was worn in a single braid, the style emphasizing her delicate bone structure.

Brian wondered if breathing was truly necessary to life; he didn't seem to do much of it around her.

He caught her hand as they walked toward the elevators, and held it firmly. It was only when the elevator opened to the lobby that he remembered a question he had wanted to ask her. "This foundation you mentioned—"

"Oh, damn! I'm glad you reminded me; I need to call the director. Why don't you get us a table while I use the phone?" She waited for his nod, then headed off toward the bank of telephones near the desk.

Brian made certain the private investigator was on duty in the lobby, then headed for the restaurant. He ran into Josh as the other man was leaving, and while they stood idly talking he asked Serena's brother about the foundation.

"Serena's?" Josh nodded. "They do a hell of a lot for sick kids. She conned me out of an endowment years ago, and Stuart too. Started it with her own money, of course, but—"

"You mean it's *her* foundation?"

"Sorry, I thought you knew." Josh looked at him rather curiously. "It's one of hers. I'm a trustee, and so is Stuart. Serena set up the policies, and of course she made sure we could help every kid with a skinned knee." He chuckled.

Brian cleared his throat carefully. "Look, I know Serena is a hell of a lot more intelligent than she lets on, but just *how much more*? I mean, foundations, policies—"

Josh looked at him seriously for a moment. There had been no constraint between the two men since Brian and Serena had become lovers, probably because Josh was an unusual kind of brother. And also because he genuinely liked Brian.

He smiled faintly. "We both know she is a multi-layered creature, our Serena." He waited for Brian's nod, then said dryly, "One of those layers just happens to be composed of a keen business mind that I would dearly love to have on any or all of my corporate boards. She graduated from Stanford, you know. Top honors. She minored in business."

"Her major?"

Josh was clearly amused. "Electronics."

Brian sighed. "Dammit."

"I don't suppose you ever asked her?"

"It never came up." Brian swore aloud. "I just assumed she'd been traipsing all over Europe having a good time. Then I found out about her foster kids. Now you tell me—What *was* she doing over there?"

"Well, she set up two foundations. And I believe there was a hospital in Switzerland. . . ."

"Hell." Brian wondered rather desperately if he'd ever get to the bottom of Serena's enigmatic person.

Josh pulled out his cigarette case and looked meditatively at its polished surface. "She uses my lawyers to go over her drafts of by-laws, organizational charters, and so forth," he said absently, "but they tell me it's sheer busywork; Serena knows what she's doing. And even though she couldn't teach Stuart about electronics, there's damn little he could teach her. She'd be a sterling asset for somebody in that business. Any business."

"Don't *you* start!" Brian snapped.

Surprised, Josh said, "Serena's been extolling her virtues?"

"No." Brian ran a hand through his hair. "The opposite, in fact. She's so closemouthed about herself, she'd give a clam rough competition!"

Josh bit back a laugh. "You sound offended."

"Well, she might have told me. At least about having a degree in electronics; she knows damn well that it's my business. It's something I just *might* have been interested in, after all. Why the hell didn't she tell me?"

Replacing his case in an inner pocket without opening it, Josh offered quietly, "Maybe she doesn't want to be accused of listing the ways in which you two are compatible. See you later, Brian."

Brian went into the restaurant and waited for Serena. He pushed Josh's last statement out of his mind, unwilling to think about it. But it hardly meant he didn't want Serena to answer his question.

He said nothing about it until they were seated across from each other, their coffee poured and their meal ordered. Then he spoke casually. "So tell me about this foundation of yours."

Serena opened her mouth, closed it, then stared at him with an absurdly guilty expression. "Josh passed me in the lobby. You talked to him, didn't you?"

"I did."

She toyed with her coffee cup. "Oh."

Since she was clearly reluctant to say anything more, Brian aired his grievances. "Foundations. Charters and by-laws. Stanford—graduated with top honors. An *electronics* major! Serena, did you deliberately play dumb with me?"

"You know I'm not dumb, Brian."

"Well, it isn't any of *your* doing that I know. I've

had to piece things together from the beginning. I've heard of hiding your light under a bushel, but, really!"

Serena smiled. "It didn't seem important, Brian. It still doesn't."

His mouth gaped in surprise as he realized that he'd come within a hair of breaking one of his own rules. If he claimed Serena's business and electronics knowledge was important, then he would also be claiming two points of compatibility between them.

Ties.

For a moment, a split second, he felt a peculiar leap of his senses. An odd, tense, cliff-hanging cessation of everything. As if the world stopped for an instant. The feeling left him bewildered and disturbed.

Serena, whether deliberately or not, didn't let him dwell on it. She began talking about the foundation, specifically about the doors being opened to little Scotty Jenkins even as they talked. She was casual, genial, offering no further information on her own involvement.

Brian accepted the conversation, responded, and tried inwardly to recapture that feeling of being on the brink of—something.

"You're a rat and a snake, and I hereby disown you!"

Josh gazed at his half sister with a raised brow, but didn't bother to dissemble. "Present a man with a puzzle and most often he'll set about solving it. If he hadn't asked me, Rena, he would have asked someone else."

"I suppose." Serena sat down on the edge of the ornamental pool, sighing. "He's taking the horses back now." She looked around the peaceful garden, then at Josh. "No pianist?"

"No, and stop changing the subject. Why are you so concerned about my answering a few innocent questions?"

"When you're walking on eggshells," she told him, "there's no such thing as an innocent question."

Josh sat down beside her. "I had a feeling it was something like that. I also have a feeling that Brian knows too."

"Knows what?" she said evasively.

"What you're doing. It's a little obvious, honey. You're trying so hard not to make demands on him."

"It'll be easier this way," she interrupted firmly.

"I don't know about that. But it's your business." Since the conversation was clearly at an end, Josh stood up. "I have a few calls to make."

"See you." Serena gazed after him. She thought in amusement that it was odd how Josh still didn't know her even after all these years. And she smiled slowly, a smile Brian had no trouble recognizing when he reached her a few moments later.

"Mona Lisa. Are you plotting?"

The enigmatic smile became a welcoming one as he sat down beside her, and she responded easily. "Just thinking about Josh, that's all. He's avoiding the pianist. I think he's afraid she bleaches her hair."

Brian looked puzzled.

"A brunette in disguise," Serena explained blandly. "It makes him nervous."

"Why do I get the feeling," Brian remarked, "that the complex and tangled minds of us mere males are open books to you?"

Serena was a little startled, and laughed before she could stop herself. "Now, that's an odd thing to say!"

He looked at her thoughtfully. "I'm not so sure. You see, Rena, there's a problem I keep stumbling over in trying to understand you."

She had the peculiar feeling that the male book wasn't the only one lying open to scrutiny. It was a feeling she hadn't often experienced in her life. "Oh, really? And what's that?"

"Well, it's been my experience that everyone has a single, basic personality trait; we all have more than one, but there's always a single trait stronger than all the rest."

"What's mine?" she asked lightly.

"That's the problem I keep running into. You have a basic desire to help people, but somehow, I don't think that's your strongest trait. You've admitted to a need to control what you can, but that isn't it either."

"I knew you were thinking about something while we were riding," Serena remarked. "Now I know what it was."

"Now you know," he agreed.

She decided rather hastily to head him off. "I think I know what your basic trait is. Discipline. You have a very orderly mind."

"Once. Long ago, maybe," he murmured.

Serena cleared her throat and got up. "Why don't we go in? If I don't soak in the tub I'll be sore tomorrow; I haven't been riding in a while."

"I'll scrub your back," he offered politely, rising and taking her hand as they headed for the building.

Serena was no fool. She knew, for instance, that a detour was simply a route one took to bypass something before getting back on the right track. In other words, neither of them forgot that Brian was busily sifting through various personality traits in an effort to discover Serena's strongest one. And it was, she thought, only a matter of time before he found it.

She honestly didn't know what would happen then. But she did know that once Brian had his answer, he would understand her completely.

Her father had pinpointed Serena's strongest trait years ago. Josh knew, but didn't *know* he knew. Which was why she could still surprise him.

Once Brian knew, she wouldn't be able to surprise him. It gave her a peculiar feeling of excitement to realize that. Although she felt anxious about the outcome, she *wanted* Brian to understand her. And he would—once he began adding things in his mind, once he pinpointed the motive behind almost every action she had taken since they had met. The trait behind all her other traits.

And Brian was working toward that target.

• • •

"Layers," he murmured. "Layers and layers." Since he was drying her body at that moment and had just pressed a warm kiss to the left of her navel, Serena didn't pay much attention.

To his words, anyway.

Some time later, he declared, "Room service," in a drained voice.

She stirred at his side and yawned. "You don't want to get dressed for dinner?"

"I don't want to move."

Serena began toying with the hairs on his chest. "The modern American male has no staying power," she observed.

"It takes nerve for you to say that. And don't lump me into a group."

"I have a lot of nerve. And you do belong to that group."

Rather abruptly Brian pulled her on top of him, staring up at her bemusedly. "Yes," he said slowly. "You do have a lot of nerve."

"I don't like your tone," she told him.

Pursuing what seemed to be an elusive trail, Brian spoke in an oddly cautious voice. "It occurs to me that you have a great deal of nerve. Meaning patience, stamina, and courage. The courage of your convictions, I think."

Serena thought that *he* had thought quite enough. She took advantage of her position to move seductively. She kissed his chin, his jaw. Obvious as the ploy was, she was certainly enjoying it. And so was Brian.

He groaned. "Don't distract me! I'm getting close."

"I'll say," she muttered, discovering somewhat gleefully that he had underestimated his body's ability to recover from exhaustion. "And I believe you were saying something about not moving?"

"Don't gloat. It's unbecoming." Then he gasped. "For heaven's sake, Serena!"

"Hmmm?"

"Oh, hell . . ."

Serena hastily reached for the ringing telephone, swearing softly. She glanced at Brian, relieved to find him still sleeping. She'd been drowsy herself, even though it was before midnight.

"Hello?" she said in a quiet voice.

"Rena, they may have found you," Josh said evenly.

She glanced again at Brian. "What makes you think so?"

"The fact," he said bitterly, "that someone was asking questions about you of the kitchen staff. They came in the back door, dammit. I'd forgotten your tendency to be known to everyone working in a hotel."

"Any descriptions?" she asked.

"The usual. Average height, average weight. Said they were reporters, and a rather impressionable busboy fell for it."

Serena chewed on her bottom lip. "What now?"

He sighed roughly. "Well, the damage is done. I think you're safe enough, particularly in Brian's room. But from now on I don't want you alone—ever. Got that?"

"I've got it. Josh, do we have to tell Brian?"

"You know the answer to that."

It was her turn to sigh. "Right."

"I mean it, Serena!"

"Don't snap. I'll be sensible."

His voice softened. "Honey, we can't be sure what their plan is. Stuart thinks it's possible they may be feeling some heat, and that means they could decide to grab you. How would Brian feel if he was caught off guard because he didn't know?"

"Yes, yes. I'll tell him in the morning."

"If you don't, I will."

"I'll tell him," she said. Then, glancing again at her sleeping lover, she added glumly, "Their timing is lousy."

"Nobody ever said they were nice guys. Good night, honey."

" 'Night, Josh."

Serena lay very still for a while, her hands resting on the tanned forearm across her waist. She frowned at the ceiling. "Plan for the unexpected," her father had always told her. Well, that was a fine bit of advice, but it wasn't very helpful at the moment.

How could one plan against a possible kidnapping?

Especially when one was the kidnapee . . .

"Why's the light on?" Brian asked sleepily.

"I like to look at your manly face," Serena replied, turning her head to do that.

"You were looking at the ceiling."

"I'm looking at you now."

"Hope you like what you see, then."

"Fishing?"

"Depends on your answer."

"I like what I see."

"I was fishing," he admitted.

Serena smiled and reached out to turn off the light before moving closer to him.

"Layers," Brian murmured, his arm tightening around her.

Eight

"Your name," Brian told her the next morning, "is perfect for you."

"Oh?"

"Yes. How the hell can you be so calm about this?"

Serena had just told him of her conversation with Josh the night before, and now resisted an urge to confide just how upset she was—and why.

"What am I supposed to be if not calm?" she asked reasonably. "There's nothing I can do about it, after all."

Brian gazed at her, thinking how absurdly young she looked in jeans and a knit top, how lovely. She was sitting in a chair by the window, with one leg thrown over its arm, regarding him with her usual tranquility.

Her usual serenity.

They might have been discussing the weather, rather than the probable presence of large men with large guns who kidnapped people and were quite likely waiting for a chance to grab her.

Suddenly, huskily, Brian said, "I'm tempted to lock the door and keep you here for the duration. Room service isn't bad." He was more than tempted; it was an urge almost too powerful to resist.

She smiled. "It might be days, Brian."

"Afraid I'll drive you crazy?"

Dispassionately she said, "I doubt you'd do that. The other way around's more likely. I'm not the easiest person to live with."

He was surprised by the statement. "I haven't had any problems so far," he observed.

"We haven't been confined in this room alone." She stood up, smiling again. "And we won't be. I refuse to be locked up, even with you, and even for my own protection."

He had expected it. Sighing, he said, "Then I don't want you out of my sight all day."

"I won't object to that."

As the day passed, Brian realized that Serena was the only one of the three of them—four, counting the P.I.—who was blithely unconcerned about her safety. She made no objection to having both him and Josh close by her all day, but didn't bother to hide her amusement.

"Why?" Brian demanded midway through the morning.

The three of them were in the hotel gift shop because Serena wanted to buy a present to send to Scotty in the hospital, and since it was a small shop, the two rather large men crowded things a bit.

"Because I can't move with you two at my elbow every minute. Wait outside?"

Josh moved to the door, chuckling, but Brian was made of sterner stuff. "That isn't what I meant, and you know it. You obviously believe you aren't in the least bit of danger. Why?"

Serena was contemplating a huge stuffed panda. "Because they know we're onto them," she answered absently.

"Come again?"

"They're pros, Brian." She handed the toy to the salesclerk and requested that it be giftwrapped, and the girl disappeared into the back of the store. "They know we're aware of them. And they know we'll be on guard—at least at first. But people can't stay on guard indefinitely, so they'll wait for a bit, until we relax."

Brian stared at her for a moment. "Plotting. You do understand that, don't you?"

"It's just common sense," she said easily.

He grimaced. "Something Josh and I are short of at the moment?"

Serena hesitated, seemed about to touch him, then merely crossed her arms beneath her breasts. "You're just worried about me," she said. "I know that."

"I wish you wouldn't—" He broke off abruptly, gazing at her with a frown.

"Wouldn't what?"

Brian sighed explosively. "Serena, I don't mind your touching me. I *like* it when you touch me." He reached out himself, brushing a strand of dark hair from her cheek, his fingers lingering to cup her neck warmly. "I like it very much," he finished huskily.

She didn't move, gazing at him with an unreadable expression in her eyes. "All right, Brian."

Frustrated, he realized that she would go on guarding her impulses to touch him. He opened his mouth to speak, but the salesclerk returned with Scotty's gift. With a smile Serena turned to deal with the details of the purchase.

Brian went to join Josh outside the door.

"Something wrong?" Serena's brother queried, studying Brian's frown.

"No." Brian looked at the younger man, then asked abruptly, "Is it true that Serena's heart condition was cured years ago?"

"It wasn't a condition," Josh said. "A defect. But, yes, it's cured. Repaired. We haven't had to worry about it for twenty years."

"There's no danger now?"

"No danger. She had a rough time of it as a kid, though. The doctors said . . ."

"Said what?"

Josh hesitated, then sighed. "That she was one hell of a fighter. She nearly died, Brian."

Brian stood staring across the lobby. Very softly, he said, "It's just wonderful the amount of information no one's thought to let me in on."

Since he had been an interested observer of Brian's developing relationship with Serena, Josh wasn't surprised to hear anger in the soft tone; he would, he decided, have felt the same way himself in Brian's place. But he tried to put things into perspective for the other man.

"Think about it for a minute. Serena was born into what most people would consider a 'privileged' life. Wealth and comfort, with a family that loved her. But in the first ten years of that life, she had to go through a hell of a lot. She was in and out of hospitals, there were several operations, and then, when she finally had her health and everything looked fine, her mother was violently killed, and she had to live under guard—literally.

"Now, those ten years might have given some people things to talk about for the rest of their lives. Not Serena. I suppose Stuart or I could have told you, but we didn't feel any need to. Neither of us had any reason to believe that her past would become important to you. And we couldn't have known that Stuart's troubles would be this serious."

"I know, I know," Brian snapped.

Josh shrugged. "A lot's happened these last few weeks. At the start you and she were strangers, and it was a simple matter of keeping her on the move and out of touch for a while. Serena, being the person she is, didn't tell you anything about herself. And in the beginning you probably weren't that curious."

"Are you kidding?" Brian stared at him, incredulous. "I was curious from the moment we met. I've never met such a ridiculous, puzzling, *baffling* woman in all my life! And she's no less baffling now, dammit. I know more about her now than I did then, but it doesn't help me understand her."

Before Josh could respond, Serena came out of the shop smiling cheerfully. "They'll deliver Scotty's present," she said. "How about tennis? Josh, where's your blonde?"

"She's not *my* blonde," Josh objected.

His remark was ignored.

"Doubles. Does she play?"

"I'll find out," Josh said, sighing, and went in search of the pianist.

With a peculiar feeling of defiance, Brian pulled a startled Serena into his arms and kissed her in full view of God and everybody.

"Did I miss something?" Serena asked when he released her.

"I don't think you miss much," Brian said musingly.

She stared up at him. "Well, then?"

"I happen to like kissing you," he said. "Sue me."

Serena couldn't help but laugh at his somewhat truculent answer. "I'm glad, but—Oh, never mind. You're in a peculiar mood, I must say."

"Not really." Brian kept an arm around her as they headed for their room to change. He had won a small victory earlier, in that neither he nor Josh thought it wise for Serena even to visit the room registered to her, so her things had been moved to Brian's room.

Changing the subject, he added, "Why're you so determined to fling that blonde at Josh?"

Serena gave him an innocent glance. "Who, me? I just want to play tennis."

Brian very quickly disregarded her statement as fiction. "Don't tell me you *know* she's really a brunette," he said.

"How would I know that?"

"A crystal ball?" he suggested, more than half serious.

"This from a man of science? I'm surprised at you."

"Serena—"

"I just want to play tennis, Brian."

Brian and Serena won the match, and Serena defeated the two men at golf the next afternoon. The blonde, whose name turned out to be Dale— "such a *dark* name," Serena observed—didn't play golf. But she enjoyed playing bridge, so that Serena instantly commandeered her to make a fourth. The two women became friends, so Dale was often in Serena's company—and in the company of the two men, who were still keeping very close to Serena.

Josh began to look hunted.

"Are you matchmaking?" Brian demanded of Serena. It was very early in the morning, they were still in bed, and Josh's hounded expression of the past few days had followed Brian into his dreams.

Serena yawned. "No," she answered rather sleepily. "I'm *un*matchmaking."

"What?"

"You heard me."

"I thought you liked Dale."

"I like her very much. But she isn't the woman for Josh."

"How," Brian asked, "can you be so sure?"

"Sequins. On her evening dresses. Even when she isn't performing."

Brian mulled that over. "Is that suppposed to answer my question?"

Serena raised herself on an elbow and stared down at Brian in the dim morning light. "Probably not. It makes sense to me, though. Let's just say that my brother isn't the sequin type; glamour doesn't hold his attention very long."

Brian reached up to toy with a strand of her dark hair. "We'll let that ride. But the point is that you're unmatchmaking. By hinting that she's really a brunette?" He shook his head. "Don't you have any faith in your brother's own judgment? If she isn't the woman for him, he'll find out by himself."

"A man obsessed," Serena told him, "is a dangerous thing. He's so anxious to avoid losing control, that he'd likely marry a blonde just to be safe. I can't let him do that, now, can I?"

"Apparently not. Look, Josh seems awfully levelheaded to me."

"He certainly is—except with regard to brunettes."

"Which is why you've hinted Dale is a brunette?"

"I'd rather see him run from her than marry in haste. The right brunette will find him one day. And soon, I think."

Brian let the subject drop. But it gave him food for thought, to consider Josh very obviously had no idea that Serena was gently maneuvering him.

Brian did a great deal of thinking. And realizing. He realized that desire didn't necessarily wane, after all, because it certainly hadn't between him and Serena. He realized that he loved waking up beside her each morning. He realized that tranquility was certainly her uppermost layer, and as each of her other layers became familiar to him, he realized that he was beginning to understand her.

But it was with grinding anxiety that Brian came to the most important realization of all, the certain understanding of Serena. And of himself.

"We've got 'em," Josh called in a satisfied tone as he approached Serena and Brian in the garden. "Stuart just called; the intelligence community finally earned its keep."

"They know who's after Daddy?" Serena asked quickly.

"They know. The wheels are turning now to start applying a discreet amount of pressure in the right places."

"Then we can go on to California?" She didn't look at Brian when she asked her brother the question.

"Stuart says in a few days. We want to make certain these guys have absorbed the reality of their situation first."

"But they're sure they know who's behind it?" Brian asked.

Josh nodded. "Quite sure." He glanced at his watch and nodded to himself. "And now I'd better go reschedule all those meetings I left up in the air. See you two at lunch." He headed back toward the building.

"He can't wait to escape the blond." Serena finally looked up at Brian, and found him watching her intently. He had not, she realized, paid attention to her observation. "It looks like it's over," she said lightly.

He nodded. "Looks like it. I'm sure you're anxious to see Stuart; it's been a while, hasn't it?"

"Yes. Yes, it has."

Steadily Brian said, "He'll expect you to live at home."

Giving herself time to think, Serena wandered over to one of the rustic wooden benches and sat down. "Actually he'll probably expect me to get a place of my own. I haven't lived at home for a long time now, Brian."

"Is that what you plan to do?"

She managed a laugh. "Unless I get a better offer."

Brian sat down beside her. "What would you consider a better offer?" he asked, still grave.

Serena, having taken great pains to be undemanding, fought an impulse to hit him with something. Then she began to wonder if Brian had made progress in trying to find her basic trait. Because if he had, he'd probably realized a few things during his search. "I've gotten used to sleeping with you," she ventured.

"What would Stuart say?"

As she glanced at him, she saw a disquieting gleam in his green eyes. Immediately alert, she proceeded cautiously. "Probably nothing. My life is my own."

"I see."

She thought he did see. And she couldn't tell from his deadpan expression what his reaction was. For one of the very few times in her life,

Serena hesitated before taking the next step forward. Finally, keeping her voice low and steady and staring straight ahead, she said, "If it's over, Brian, tell me."

"I wonder if it'd do any good," he replied musingly.

He was, Serena decided with an irrepressible inner laugh, ruining her noble scene. She forgave him for it; heaven knew he'd earned the right. Still, doggedly, she stuck to her lines.

"You never made promises," she conceded with quiet reluctance. "I know that. And if I hadn't— Well, I forced your hand, didn't I? But I knew what I was doing. I'm not a child, after all. You've been honest from the first, Brian, and I appreciate that."

Politely he said, "I'm glad."

Serena felt his eyes on her profile, but refused to look at him. She had a feeling that if she did, it would bring down the curtain early. He had it now, or at least part of it, she was sure.

She artistically shaped a quaver and threaded it through her voice. "I'll—I'll move my things back to the other room."

"I'm almost tempted to let you do that. But I'd hate to put you to the bother of seducing me again."

Curtain, she thought with real amusement. But it was just the end of an act, not the play. She mentally chided herself for underestimating Brian's quickness, a mistake she wouldn't make a second time. Then she folded her hands in her lap, turned her head to gaze at him limpidly, and said very gently, "Oh, it wouldn't be a bother."

There was a flicker of satisfaction in his eyes,

and he lifted a brow at her. "Wasn't I supposed to figure it out?"

Serena shrugged delicately. "That was always a possibility, of course. And one must always take possibilities into account."

He nodded with all the air of a man deep in thought. "I'm sure. You would have covered all the bases. So if I'd said it was over, you would have gone on being quite pathetically noble?"

"For a while."

"And then?"

"Oh, sad, I think. Brokenhearted."

"And thereby rendering me ripe for a second seduction?"

"Something like that."

"I see. But I *did* figure it out, Serena. So, what now?"

She smiled at him. "Well, that depends on you. I can't believe you want it to be over. You don't, do you?"

"No," he said dryly. "In spite of everything, I don't."

"Then there's no problem."

"I wish I could believe that." He stared at her. "But I have this uncomfortable feeling that even though I've figured out *something*, I still don't have the whole picture."

She smiled again, gently.

Brian began to understand Josh's recent feelings. There was something disquieting in feeling hunted—and not being sure for what reason or by whom.

"Are you still altar-bound?" he demanded suddenly.

Serena leaned over, slid her arms up around his neck, and kissed him.

"That's no answer," he said hoarsely.

"Brian," she said in a reasonable tone, "have I ever—ever—been demanding?"

He pulled her over onto his lap, saying irritably, "No. But, yes—somehow."

"That isn't very clear."

"I'm not surprised!" he retorted.

Serena fought an urge to giggle. "Brian, I could hardly deliver you to the altar bound and gagged, could I? And even if I could, you wouldn't be able to say the vows. Obviously there is no way I could marry you against your will. So what are you worried about?"

"My will." He sighed. "You seem to have a knack for eroding it. Like water dripping on a stone."

She linked her fingers together behind his neck. "You're the master of your fate. The captain of your soul."

"And you," he said, "are three parts sorceress."

"Is it a crime that I happen to realize what I want and intend to go after it? All right, perhaps I was a bit underhanded—"

"*Perhaps?*" He was astonished.

"Brian, think about it! The jealousy ploy didn't work. And since I'd very stupidly let it slip that I'd never had a lover, you weren't willingly *about* to be the first. What was I supposed to do—tell you very honestly that I was willing to have an affair? I tried, but that didn't work either."

He objected. "You did no such thing. You said, 'Let's pretend,' *and* looked like a puppy about to

IN SERENA'S WEB • 149

be kicked when you said it! I'd have felt guilty as hell—and did, for that matter."

"So I had to seduce you."

She also had the knack, Brian thought, for making her own reasoning sound perfectly clear. But, being an intelligent man, he didn't point that fact out to her.

"You need a keeper."

"Are you applying?"

"No, dammit."

Unperturbed, Serena grinned at him. "Then just go on being my lover, Brian."

"Serena, look me in the eye and answer one question honestly. Truthfully. Will you do that?"

"I'll have to hear it first."

That didn't surprise him. "Do you understand—really understand—that I don't want to get married?"

"Yes," she answered promptly. "I understand that. Now, can we go on being lovers?"

"You're shameless."

"I know. Answer the question."

Brian devoutly hoped it was his own secret that he couldn't have said no to save his life. However, since she was sitting on his lap, he doubted it. "Yes. I suppose."

Meekly she said, "Thank you."

Brian kissed her quickly, then got her off his lap and back onto the bench beside him. "One thing you're not too convincing at," he said, "is being humble."

"I'll work on it." With everything back on track again, Serena smiled at him. She had realized that Brian didn't quite have it yet. But he was getting there. Eventually he'd discover what drove her. Now . . . if he could only discover what drove *him*, everything would be fine.

Brian eyed her thoughtfully. "Tell me something. Have you ever performed a completely spontaneous action? Or is everything planned?"

She returned his gaze and decided to drop a gentle hint. "The actions are always spontaneous, Brian. It's the situations that are planned."

"I don't get it."

"Well, for instance, my falling in love with you was a completely spontaneous action. I would hardly have chosen to do so if I'd been given the choice—not with men trying to get at Daddy through me. But, having fallen in love with you, I just naturally arranged the situation."

He blinked. "God, you're frightening."

"I'm being honest."

"Where've I heard that before?"

"I do love you, you know."

Disarmed, he could only stare at her. And as he stared at her, it occurred to him with shocking simplicity that he loved her. More, he was *in* love with her. In love with her surface tranquility and the boiling caldron of emotions underneath. In love with her compassion and her need to control and even her damned plotting. In love with gray eyes and a lovely face, and with a passion that matched his own. In love with the glance that could summon waiters, bellmen, and skycaps, and a voice that was always soft and gentle.

He was enchanted with the troublesome sprite he had fished out of the muddy Mississippi, and the unrepentant woman he had bailed out of jail early one morning. Captivated by the woman who had used her half brother in an effort to make him jealous. Bewitched by a seductress who had come to him in the gray, silent hours of the morning.

It occurred to him that he had loved her for some time.

Brian, his mind whirling, started to tell her that. But an intruding voice claimed his attention, and he looked aside to find one of the bellmen addressing him.

"Mr. Ashford—telephone call for you."

Brian nodded and rose to his feet, gazing once more at Serena.

"I'll wait here for you." She smiled.

After a moment he nodded again and headed for the hotel.

Alone in the garden, Serena swore softly. Her heart was pounding against her ribs, and she had to force herself to take calming breaths. Had his sudden silence, his shocked expression, meant what she thought? And if so—damn the unknown caller!

It just wasn't *fair* that Brian should be called away from her now.

She brooded silently. It was temporary, of course, but maddening nonetheless. For the first time she allowed herself to think of the future with certainty, and that felt just wonderful.

If everything went according to plan.

Brian, feeling that he was moving by rote, went to the desk to take his call. Inattentively he said, "Hello?"

It took several long seconds for him to realize there was no one on the line. He stared at the receiver for a moment, then beckoned the nearby desk clerk. "I thought I had a call."

"Yes, sir. No one's on the line?"

"No one." He hung up the receiver, vaguely troubled. Shrugging, he left the desk.

Josh was just coming from the elevators. "Are we ready to have lunch?" he demanded. "I'm starving."

"Sure. Serena's in the garden." A bell went off in Brian's mind, and he stopped abruptly. "I just got a call," he muttered. "But there was no one on the line." He felt strangely light-headed, cold. His mind moved sluggishly. An awful certainty grew within him.

"I'll get—" Josh broke off as Brian's words sank in, and he stared at the other man's white face. His own face drained of color. "There hasn't been time for them to get the word," he breathed. "They don't know it's off!"

Brian barely heard the last word. He was running for the garden, dread clenching his heart, and the overwhelming thought in his mind was that he had waited too long to tell her.

Serena wasn't conscious of her aloneness. Nor, a little later, did she immediately realize that she had company. She had forgotten that the danger of her being alone was still present, that it took time to call off dogs on a hunt.

She had forgotten to be aware, to be wary.

But her instincts prevailed, and when heavy

hands fell on her shoulders, those instincts warned that the hands were unfriendly. Her body reacted instantly, twisting, surging away from the unfriendly grasp.

More hands grabbed her, strong hands, and in the instant it took for her to react, to lash out at her attackers, a white pad was pressed to her face, covering her nose and mouth.

Chloroform.

Her mind identified the odor, and as she quickly succumbed, her body went limp and helpless.

And her last thought had been the realization that they'd let down their guard too soon.

Nine

Gone.

An icy calm came over Brian when they found Serena gone. He and the private investigator—both caught off guard—searched the garden and grounds, while Josh raced to alert Stuart. He agreed with the P.I. that they'd found no signs, no clues as to where Serena had been taken.

In Josh's room Brian listened silently while Serena's brother gave instructions for the P.I. to try to find out if anyone had seen Serena get into a car and could give a description of the vehicle, and then sent him from the room. When Brian finally spoke, it was in a quiet voice.

"What now?"

Josh looked at him searchingly. "First, we can't call in the police or FBI; it'd be certain death for Serena if we did." He pulled his cigarette case out and opened it.

"May I?"

"I didn't think you smoked," Josh answered, surprised.

"I don't." Brian accepted the light. His hands were steady.

Josh lighted his own cigarette, and expelled the smoke in a short burst. "Second—unless we get a call, there isn't a hell of a lot we can do ourselves."

"And if we get a call?"

"If Serena has any idea where she is, she'll try to tell us somehow."

"What if we don't get a call?"

"There's still hope," Josh said quickly. "The kidnappers will get in touch with their bosses to announce their success. We're assuming the bosses don't yet know we're onto them. If we're correct, they'll probably contact Stuart, who will make certain they understand the situation. If the bosses *do* know we've discovered them, it's entirely possible they'll cancel the operation and give orders to release Serena."

Brian smoked for a few moments in silence. Then he said in a cool tone, "Even if Serena's seen their faces?"

Josh hesitated for a fraction of a second. "Even then. A kidnapping can, if all parties agree, be kept quiet. It doesn't have to end in murder."

Brian was studying the glowing end of his cigarette. "Correct me if I'm wrong. There are . . . buffers between the dogs and the masters."

Feeling quite savage himself, Josh silently approved the allusion. He nodded. "Right."

"Suppose," Brian suggested, "the dogs don't like their orders. They're the ones in the hot spot, the ones who would have to face a kidnapping rap. Suppose they operate on the theory that a dead witness can't testify against them, and they disobey orders."

Josh drew a deep breath. "Cheerful bastard, aren't you?"

Brian waited.

"Then she's dead," Josh said flatly. "But the chances are against that happening. These particular masters choose their dogs well, and pay them accordingly. And they don't pay big bucks for stupidity. If the dogs follow orders, they're taken care of; if they disobey, they're very likely dead themselves. They *know* that, Brian."

"I hope they do." Brian studied his cigarette again, then stubbed it out. In a peculiarly conversational tone he added, "Because if they don't know it, if we don't get Serena back alive and completely unmarked, they'll never see the inside of a jail."

Having felt the punishment of Brian's fist after what had been, relatively speaking, a case of mild frustration, Josh understood completely. He understood that after Brian got through with them, Serena's captors undoubtedly would see nothing.

Nothing at all.

Serena woke to darkness. Her head hurt, her mouth was dry, she was cramped and uncomfortable, and she was quite thoroughly bound and gagged. She was also, she suspected, in the trunk of a car.

A moment of cautious testing was enough to convince her that whoever had tied the knots behind her back had known what he was doing; she couldn't loosen the rope. She abandoned the attempt, unwilling to waste her energy. Even though she was blinded by darkness and stuffed into a car's trunk, she tried to gather some impression of where she was.

She refused to allow her own terror to control her. Never. Never that. It was self-defeating.

Easily said, of course. She *was* terrified.

Fiercely shoving that realization away, she concentrated on listening, on feeling. And she knew after a moment that the car was stopped. Parked? she wondered. The engine *was* running, and she could hear something else. A rumble. As much to keep her mind occupied as to learn something, Serena concentrated on that sound.

Then the car moved, briefly. She could still hear the rumble, she realized. The car stopped, and the engine died, and Serena listened closely to voices that sounded muffled and curt.

When the trunk lid was lifted, she closed her eyes tightly against the bright light. The sun was still high in the sky; either it was the next day or, as she supposed, she hadn't been unconscious for very long.

Hands moved behind her, and she barely felt the sudden release as her wrists and ankles were untied, since she'd lost all feeling in her hands and feet several minutes before.

"Don't touch the gag," a deep voice ordered sharply. "And don't give us any trouble, or we'll tie you up again."

As she was lifted from the trunk Serena could make no effort to resist. Each of the two men took hold of an upper arm to support her. She was still so numb, she couldn't have struggled effectively if she had wanted to.

They hustled her into a building, and she had only a moment to try to absorb some impression of where she was. Recognition woke in her mind, and she held on to it fiercely. It wasn't much, but it was something.

The building was old, and smelled of disuse and decay. Serena, dwarfed between her large captors, was taken into a small, windowless room. The furnishings consisted of a rickety table on which sat a telephone, incongruous in its shiny newness.

Serena pulled the gag from her mouth as they released her, a test that she apparently passed, since they made no objection. They wanted her to talk, she realized, and her mind began working frantically. Feeling was returning to her hands and feet, she could feel the sensation of needles stabbing, but she was still virtually helpless. She swallowed, her throat still dry and painful, and looked for the first time at her captors.

They were big men, powerful, but with their nondescript hair and eyes, and their average faces, Serena would have a hard time describing them. They were as alike as bookends, dressed casually to fit in just about anywhere. Both watched her intently, but there was no savagery in their expressions.

No threat.

Serena was not particularly reassured.

"There's no need for you to be afraid, Miss Jameson," one of the bookends said in a voice he probably imagined to be soothing. "Just do what we say and don't make trouble. We're going to spend a little time together, that's all. You'll be back in your hotel by nightfall."

"We want you to call the hotel," the other book-end said curtly. "And tell Mr. Long and Mr. Ashford that you're all right. Tell them not to do anything foolish, like calling the police. Your health depends on their caution."

It should have sounded melodramatic, instead it sounded frightening.

Serena kept her expression as haughty as possible. "You're going to regret this," she said coldly, playing the part she had already selected. "When my father finds out—"

"Make the call," the second bookend ordered brusquely.

Serena walked easily to the table and picked up the receiver, placing a call to the hotel. She asked for Josh's room, having decided that both he and Brian would be there waiting for just such a call. And they were.

"Josh?"

"Serena!" His tone of voice revealed how relieved he felt, also how concerned he was. "Are you all right? Can you say anything?"

She looked at the second bookend, not surprised to find he had a wicked-looking automatic weapon pointed at her. She forced a sarcastic laugh. "Oh, I'm fine. I haven't felt this good since Jackson. They tell me," she added, "to warn you not to be incautious. No police. My . . . my health depends on it."

One of the men stepped toward her, and Serena tried quickly to say what she hoped wouldn't be her last words to her brother. "Tell Brian—" The receiver was taken away from her and replaced firmly. She was sorry she hadn't been able to finish the message, but the calm of her captors eased some of her worry. They hadn't noticed the vitally important "throwaway" line in her message.

She hoped Brian would understand.

The first bookend complimented her politely. "Very good, Miss Jameson." Then he looked at the second man. "Take her out. I'll make the call."

Serena obeyed the slight wave of the gun, and preceded the second bookend out of the room. She found herself in a huge space, the shadowy interior illuminated only by faint light coming through the dirt-encrusted windows. A warehouse, she realized. There was a single chair beneath a naked, glaring lightbulb suspended from the high ceiling. Beside the chair was a small table that was bare except for a Thermos bottle.

She didn't like the thought of what might be in that bottle.

Looking at the second bookend with arrogant astonishment that was only partly feigned, she said, "Surely you jest."

Her calculated sneer had its effect; he scowled at her. "Sit," he ordered.

Serena lifted one delicate brow at him and said, "It's obvious you need to associate with a better class of victim. I never attended obedience school, so please refrain from the canine commands."

She crossed her arms over her breasts and stared at him with what she hoped looked like fearless scorn.

Brian was on his feet, staring at Josh. He was so still, he might have been carved from granite. "Well?"

"She's all right, but we're not to call the police. She sounded fine, Brian." Josh decided not to mention that Serena's last words had been cut off with chilling abruptness. That was not something the other man needed to hear right now.

"Could she say anything?"

Josh frowned. "Yes, she could. And did. She said she hadn't had this much fun since Jackson. It has to mean something to one of us. I've never been anyplace called Jackson with her, so the clue must have been meant for you. Which Jackson? Mississippi?"

Brian scowled. "No," he said. "Not there, I'm sure. We didn't pass through Jackson, Mississippi."

Josh ran a hand through his dark hair. "Well, then? There *must* have been a Jackson sometime during the trip, or she wouldn't have said what she did. It has to mean something she'd expect you to remember. Think!"

"Wait." Brian nodded. "Now I remember. It was Tennessee. Jackson, Tennessee. It was a special stop, just for one day. We had to go out of our way, I remember, but she insisted."

"Why? What was special about it?" Josh tried to think clearly. "What did she want to see there?"

"She said—she'd always been intrigued by the ballad of Casey Jones."

After a moment Josh said, "All I remember of it is that he was an engineer."

"The railroad museum," Brian said, his voice quickening for the first time. "It was the only thing we saw. Josh, wherever she's being kept—there are *trains*!"

"Trains?"

Instantly both men bent over the huge county map spread on Josh's bed, searching for railroad tracks and perhaps a freight yard.

If Serena had allowed fear to control her, she would have been completely helpless. She knew that. So, to take her mind off her quivering insides, she had been plotting from the moment she'd come to.

Her scheme was necessarily incomplete, since she couldn't know when or how a rescue attempt would be made. But she did know one *would* be made. She knew her father, knew Josh—and knew Brian.

They'd find her.

And when they did, Serena would be ready.

Serena was playing her role carefully. With every scornful look, every haughty gesture, and every arrogant word, she was carefully painting a picture of a rich man's spoiled, contemptuous, self-assured daughter. A hothouse flower, cultivated in gentle soil and raised to be an ornament.

She was clearly, obviously confident that this was merely an uncomfortable interlude, an inconvenience soon to be dealt with by her loving father. She was annoyed, insolent. She complained of her surroundings, the dirt and darkness, with disdain. She was bored, restless.

Serena was—shrewdly—betting that these men had been told next to nothing about her. But even if she were wrong, there were certain things about her that they simply could not know, thanks to her father's cautious foresight.

They couldn't know she was hell on wheels, gifted with fast reflexes and a cool mind.

The role helped her to keep her mind off the very strong possibility that she could be killed. Like Josh, she had a good idea of how the kidnapping was meant to be handled. The first bookend, she knew, had called his boss—who was most likely not the top man. But the top man, or men, would be notified that she was in custody.

Her two bookends were clearly expecting another call, probably to be told that Stuart had caved in. She amended that thought. The bookends were functionaries only, who probably wouldn't be told what was behind this. So, the phone call they were waiting for was to let them know that they could release their captive.

But Serena knew that wouldn't be the call they'd get. Whether or not her bookends were apprised of just what was going on, the top men in this knew, or would shortly know, that Stuart would never cave in. They'd know that they'd been traced, and were being watched most carefully. Holding Serena would do them no good at all, and killing her would bring definite trouble down on their heads.

Serena also knew that what happened then was . . . well, problematic. The top men could, if they wished, simply give the expected order. And if the bookends trusted their employers to make certain they wouldn't face a kidnapping rap, the order would be obeyed.

But the possible variations on that were endless.

Her captors could decide—indeed, might long since have decided—that leaving behind a live witness to testify to a kidnapping wasn't very smart. Or very healthy. They could decide to save their own hides. To kill her, dispose of the body, and head for parts unknown.

Serena could be reasonably certain that the original orders had been to take her, but keep her alive and release her when so ordered. Stuart would not, after all, do so much as a day's work for the men who had ordered, or allowed, the death of his daughter. After all, she was all he had left.

And it was doubtful the orders would differ now, because the top men had a great deal to lose in having her killed, and a great deal to gain, relatively speaking, by returning her alive. They were being watched, and just because there might be little or no courtroom proof against them didn't mean they wouldn't pay, and pay heavily, for having her killed.

So what it all boiled down to was that Serena's safety depended, curiously enough, on the integrity of her captors. On whether or not they would carry out orders they'd been paid to carry out.

Serena didn't want to count on that. It would have been, she knew, insanely foolish to do so.

So she complained occasionally, and made the expected threats against her captors, and pushed them as far as she dared. She was playing her role perfectly.

Now she could only wait for Brian and Josh to find her.

Josh was driving, following the route they'd selected, while Brian frowned over the map he was holding.

"There are five major rail-freight lines and Amtrak," Brian said. "How can we be sure this is where they're holding her? D'you really think—?"

Nodding, Josh pointed briefly to the area on the map circled in red. "It has to be near a freight line," he said resolutely, fighting to convince himself as well as Brian. "They have to have somewhere to keep her; a warehouse would be less dangerous than an empty car, I'd say. An abandoned warehouse, most likely; they wouldn't want to have some passerby or security guard stumble on them accidentally.

"According to the Chamber of Commerce and the contacts that Paul, our private investigator, has in town, the freight yard we've circled is the only one with empty warehouses nearby. The only one that isn't used anymore. It fits, Brian."

"D'you think they'll have the car hidden?"

"Under cover, probably, but we should be able to find it. Paul's certain they were driving a blue sedan. If they didn't change cars . . . we'll be able to find that, at least."

"You told him not to crowd us?" Brian glanced over his shoulder at the car behind them.

"He knows. He'll back us up once we get inside, but he'll take no action on his own until Rena's safe."

They had already discussed how they were going to handle the situation.

After a moment Brian said quietly, "We can't allow any shooting, and we know they'll be armed. No matter how we go in, they'll probably have Serena close, within reach. They'll use her as a shield to stand us off or to get away." He was still troubled by the plan they'd decided on.

"Not if she's ready for us," Josh said calmly. "Serena's never been passive in her life; she won't expect us to do all the work." He sent Brian a strained grin. "She was taught early to have little faith in knights in shining armor. By now I'll bet she's convinced the dogs that she's the frailest, most spoiled flower this side of the Civil War. It is, to put it mildly, a wrong impression."

Brian stirred uneasily. "I know you said she was trained in self-defense, but if she takes them on by herself, or makes the wrong move once we show up—"

"She won't. Serena isn't out to prove anything, Brian. She won't try to take them on alone, or try to disarm them when we come busting in. Count on that. Her first priority will be to make damned sure she doesn't get in our way. She knows very well that the cavalry's rescue can be screwed up if someone gets caught in the cross fire."

With a faint smile Brian said, "Sounds like you're counting on her to think clearly. Will she?"

Seriously Josh said, "Stuart's a farsighted man; he knew there was the possibility of something like this happening years ago. Especially after Mother was killed. So he taught Serena and me things most kids never have to learn. If it comes right down to it, I suppose our childhood 'drills' are partly responsible for Rena's highly developed ability to plan ahead. Stuart would suddenly say, 'What if—' and detail some elaborate situation. We had to get ourselves safely out of it. Rena was good at it, damned good. Nine times out of ten she not only got herself out of the mythical situation, but, in doing so, thought of a solution even Stuart hadn't considered."

He sighed. "I'm not saying she isn't scared, or that she isn't in shock. The thing is, she'll give in to the fear and shock only when the danger's past. She's amazingly cool-headed under stress."

Brian believed him. He understood Serena now, understood her completely. He knew the woman he loved would never give in to panic, because it was totally alien to her.

How he loved her. . . .

Realizing they were getting close, the men fell silent. They found the freight yard and circled it once, warily, from a distance. Josh parked the car, and he and Brian watched the P.I. park his own car about a hundred yards away. They both looked carefully at the group of buildings in the distance. They were old, clearly abandoned, most of them half falling down or leaning one way or the other.

Brian pointed suddenly. "There. Is that a glint of blue? At the corner of that building?"

"Looks like it." Abruptly Josh sounded his horn in a quick pattern.

Brian, who had started to object, caught on quickly and remained silent. He realized that the sound would not be unusual; there was considerable traffic around the area, and other car horns sounded intermittently. He also realized that he knew the pattern.

"S-O-S. She knows Morse?"

"She knows. And if she heard that, she'll be ready."

"If she didn't?"

"If she didn't, she still has reflexes like a cat. Come on, let's very quietly find some way into that building."

Serena heard the distant horn. Sending another scornful glance at her captors, she realized they hadn't heard—or hadn't listened. Which was just fine.

She had nearly exhausted her repertoire of snide comments, but managed a few more biting ones as she paced in a circle near the table and chair.

With great care she had gotten the two men accustomed to her bored, restless pacing. She walked, she glared at them, she picked up the Thermos and put it back down disdainfully, she complained in annoyance about a broken fingernail. They leaned against iron support posts and watched her, emotionless.

Serena estimated that neither one of them could move fast enough to catch her instantly, but she also realized that there was no cover for her, no place to hide, except in the shadows along the walls. She marked the spot in her mind, trusting in her own speed more than anything else.

She paced, she muttered. She listened intently, ears straining.

All she wanted, all she hoped for, was a split second's warning. Just an instant that would give her time to distract her captors somehow and make certain they couldn't get their hands on her.

When the moment came, she was so ready for it that she reacted at once.

The phone in the small office shrilled suddenly, and as one of the bookends swiveled toward the sound, something came crashing through two of the dirty windows. Both men were caught off guard, startled, thrown off balance physically and mentally.

Serena picked up the Thermos and threw it hard at the bookend who was turning and reaching for his gun, and then she dived with all her strength toward the shadowy wall.

And all her strength was too much, as it turned out.

Rena was only dimly aware of things happening around her. Yells, crashes and thumps, grunts, and gunshots. Then she heard a hoarse voice and felt someone moving her, holding her, touching her with warm and gentle hands, saying something over and over to her, something she couldn't quite hear and didn't worry about. She instinctively felt safe.

She floated for a while, content.

Then she was being moved again, and there were new voices, and something was being done to her head. It hurt like hell, she realized. She was annoyed by the pain, and muttered a fretful complaint that emerged as a whisper. She vaguely heard someone mention "an injection for shock," and wanted to tell the person with the officious voice that she wasn't in shock. Her head hurt and she wanted to be left alone to suffer, but she was given no choice in the matter. She felt a prick in her arm, and she immediately lost all interest in the situation.

When Rena woke, it was with customary abruptness. She instantly sat up, and said quite clearly, "Of all the stupid—" Then she winced and lifted her hand to touch her forehead and the gauze pad taped there.

"I'll say."

The voice came from her left. She turned her head carefully and gazed at Josh as he sat slumped in a chair by her bed. Brian's bed, she realized. She was in his room.

"I'll say," he repeated dryly, "it was stupid. I mean, to knock yourself out in your moment of glory . . . !"

"How did I know the wall was so close?" she asked reasonably. "It was dark. There were shadows. I couldn't see very well. And besides, it didn't feel like glory. Reality is a lot more scary than theory, let me tell you, and damnably hard to control. Where's Brian?"

"I sent him down to get something to eat a few minutes ago. He's been sitting here for hours, and he was starting to talk to himself."

"Oh." She tried to recall events, and realized everything was pretty unclear, especially what occurred after she'd dived into the wall. "What happened to the bookends?"

Her half brother didn't need the question clarified, although he grinned faintly at the word she used for her captors. "They're in safe hands. Bound, gagged, and waiting in the warehouse with Paul. Stuart's intelligence friends want a crack at them. If they can speak coherently, which I doubt."

"Aren't they feeling well?" Serena asked interestedly, banking pillows behind her and discovering that someone had changed her clothes, putting on her violet nightgown. She hoped that someone had been Brian.

Josh grinned again. "I don't think so."

"You and Brian?" she guessed.

"I didn't get much of a chance." The slightly bruised condition of his knuckles seemed to indicate a slight exaggeration, but his face was solemn.

She blinked. "You mean Brian—?"

"He went berserk," Josh said dryly.

Serena's eyes widened. "Brian? But I've never seen him lose his temper, and he's had plenty of chances to. I've driven him crazy for weeks!"

"Did I say he lost his temper?" Josh looked and sounded quite mild.

"Well, then?"

"I said he went berserk." Reminiscently Josh elaborated. "We crashed in—and there you lay, apparently lifeless. I suppose Brian could be forgiven for instantly assuming you'd been treated badly at best, and that you were dead at worst. He acted accordingly. One of the dogs was whirling around looking wonderfully surprised, and the other seemed to be trying to get rid of a Thermos. Were you responsible for that, by the way?" he added curiously.

"I threw it. Just before I dived."

"Nice going." Josh nodded approvingly. "He apparently caught it by reflex and was trying to unload it at about the time we got to our feet."

"And then?"

"And then things started happening rather quickly. Brian, as I said, took one look at your fallen body and went berserk. I've never seen a man move so fast in my life. One of the guys got off a couple of shots, but missed. Brian took his gun away from him—it looked pathetically easy, although I know damned well it wasn't—and then lit into them both. If I hadn't managed to make sure you were still among the living and convinced him of that, he would've killed them." Josh didn't add that he'd nearly been decked himself in the attempt.

After a moment Serena began to smile. "I suppose it must have been his sense of responsibility working overtime," she murmured. "Or something."

"Or something," Josh agreed gravely. "The man obviously has a ridiculously short fuse. Anyway, we left the dogs to Paul, gathered you up, and came back here. The hotel doctor said you didn't have a concussion, but he thought you should sleep for a while. Brian sat with you until I threatened to get the doctor after *him* a few minutes ago."

"You called Daddy?"

"First thing." Josh smiled. "He was, predictably, calm. Brian talked to him, as a matter of fact. Or, rather, yelled at him. He didn't make much sense. I took the phone away from him and explained to Stuart that you were alive and had done great credit to him as a teacher of the art of survival. He said to tell you that he loves you, and to please come home before you get into any more trouble."

Serena took a deep breath. "Then, it's over?"

"It's over."

"Did Brian say anything?"

Josh smiled slowly. "Yes, he said something. And repeated variations of it all the way back here. But I think you should hear it from him, don't you?"

"I certainly do." Serena smiled, tossed back the covers, and stood, being carefully still until the dizziness subsided. It went away quickly; Serena had a hard head. "Can you give me a few minutes before you tell him I'm awake, Josh? I want to shower."

Her brother got to his feet and stretched. "Sure." He started for the door, then paused and turned back to her. "Serena . . ."

"Yes, Josh?"

"You couldn't have *known* it would turn out this way. I mean, not in the beginning, when you were plotting to make him jealous."

Serena gazed at him with limpid, mildly astonished eyes. "Josh, how *could* I have known?"

"That's what I thought." He shook his head, and left the room. But he was vaguely—just vaguely—dissatisfied with her answer.

Smiling a little, she headed for the bathroom. Serena took her shower, feeling elated and impatient to see Brian. She was finished, dressed in a fresh nightgown, and brushing her hair before the mirror above the dresser, when he came in.

For a moment they stared at each other. Brian

looked a little tired. His knuckles were considerably more bruised than Josh's had been, and a swelling along his left cheekbone testified to the fact that at least one of the bookends had managed a bit of self-defense.

Serena put down her brush and turned to face him, saying softly, "It isn't often these days that a woman can be saved from peril. How do I thank you?"

"Marry me," he said deeply.

She swallowed hard and managed a shaky laugh. "You aren't the marrying kind. You told me so. The debt isn't worth such a sacrifice."

Silently Brian came to her. He touched her face with his hand, his lips seeking hers. He kissed her with passion and relief and tenderness, and with a possessiveness Serena could feel branding her indelibly. She felt herself lifted into his arms and carried a short distance, and when she opened her eyes she discovered that Brian was leaning back against the headboard of the bed and she was in his lap.

"I love you," he said softly.

Ten

Serena felt as if she had just released a breath she'd held for a very long time. She rested her forehead against his briefly, her hands at his neck. She smiled slowly, gazing into shining green eyes. "I love you too."

"And you'll marry me?" he asked huskily.

In a grave tone she asked, "Are you sure about this, Brian? We've been through a lot today, and I'd hate to catch you with your guard down."

"Answer the question."

"Of course I'll marry you, darling."

He smiled, brushing a strand of hair from her face.

"You knew I would," she observed critically.

"I knew."

Serena smiled, and waited. She was reasonably sure of just what else he knew, but she wanted to hear it from him.

Brian held her tightly and kissed her again. When he finally drew back to stare down at her, his eyes were very bright. "I've figured out a couple of things," he said.

"What things?"

"Us." He smiled crookedly. "You and me."

Serena laughed unsteadily. "You first."

He agreed with a nod. "Me. Well, the shock of nearly losing you made me realize something. I was so hell-bent on not having a future with you that I never stopped to ask myself a simple question. I never asked myself *why* it was impossible."

"And now?"

"Now I know the answer. You were right about the strong habits of bachelors, Rena. In my twenties I made a decision—a logical one. I was going to build a company, and I didn't have the time or emotional energy for a lasting relationship. So I established a certain lifestyle based on that decision. After a while it became sheer, blind habit."

He shook his head, amazed at himself. "And that habit was so strong, I wouldn't let myself realize I was in love with you."

Her smile glowed.

Brian kissed her quickly, hard. "And you knew that. You've known it all along. I'll bet you've known since the day—" His gaze was suddenly speculative. "When did I fall in love with you, Rena?"

She didn't hesitate. "The morning you bailed me out of jail."

He laughed, delighted. "I was sure you'd know! But how did I give myself away? I was mad as hell that morning."

"Yes, you were." She laughed softly. "You swore like the devil. But before you started swearing, you hugged me. You didn't even seem to realize you'd done it. I knew then."

"So you decided to marry me?"

"I loved you too," she said solemnly.

"But I was the victim of my blind habit."

She nodded. "You certainly were. And you weren't even aware that it was a habit. It seemed to me that what you needed was a shaking. And since I could hardly shake you physically, well . . ."

"You shook me emotionally. By very sweetly announcing that you'd decided to marry Josh, and making me believe you, dammit. And then you shook me further by asking me to teach you the arts of seduction, after innocently confiding that you were a virgin." Dispassionately he added, "Lord, you're ruthless."

"You turned me down," she reminded him.

"And you," he retorted dryly, "claimed to have lost control, and contritely admitted your plotting. You admitted to loving me. You stopped flirting. You trapped me in a web so devious, I didn't know which way was up!"

"But I'd stopped plotting," she said innocently.

Brian smiled. "My darling, you never stopped plotting."

Serena smiled her enigmatic Mona Lisa smile, and he nodded firmly.

"Never. Having maneuvered me neatly until I could barely think straight, you then dropped your bombshell. Our relationship wasn't going to progress—obviously. You'd be hurt eventually, and I'd feel guilty, and so, stalemate. But we could pretend. And you very affectingly offered to do just that, which gave me one hell of a sleepless night, witch!"

"I had to seduce you," she admitted.

"And very nicely, too."

"Thank you."

Brian cleared his throat. "Now. We had reached the turning point in our relationship, and all according to plan. We were lovers, and you wasted hardly a moment in absolving me of guilt. Presumably so that I wouldn't turn into a gibbering idiot."

Serena giggled.

He went on. "After which you embarked on the final phase of your plan. Which was: no demands. You were so damned *un*demanding that I was always conscious of it."

Deciding a comment was called for, Serena said gravely, "It seemed to me that a man would realize what he *really* wanted if he was given what he *thought* he wanted."

"So you gave me what I thought I wanted. A nice, uncomplicated affair."

"It *was* what you thought you wanted. No strings. No ties."

"And that was when my mind—very belatedly, I must say—started to work again."

"What sparked it?" she asked curiously.

Brian could hardly help but grin at the question. "When I found out about your foundations and your keen business mind. Josh, who was responsible for most of the facts I was trying to piece together, said something once about your being made up of layers and layers. Well, I kept seeing your different layers. But I had the odd impression that the *order* of the layers was wrong, in my mind, I mean. I'd started with a false assumption, you see. Something else Josh said—and which he believes—was that your basic core was one of trusting vulnerability."

"And you don't think so?" she asked, wounded.

He grinned again. "No, darling, I certainly do not!"

Serena tried to look offended, but laughed instead. "All right. And so?"

"When I decided that perhaps your brother didn't know you as well as he thought he did, I started to make progress. I started adding together the pieces I was certain of, the facts I knew to be true."

"Which were?"

"First and foremost was the fact that Stuart was perfectly content to let you run your own life. He's no fool, which meant that neither were you. That, plus your degree and your involvement with foundations and the like, added up to more than a brilliant mind. It added up to brilliance, yes, but also common sense, logic, and a knack for organization."

"I see."

"Yes. And since I'd seen ample evidence of it, I also knew that you controlled what you could, when you could. Another point: You had an uncanny knack for understanding people, which springs from genuine interest and genuine compassion."

"Thank you."

"You're welcome. At that point I started arranging your layers in my mind. Don't laugh!"

"It sounds funny. Sorry. You were saying?"

"Layers. I started with the surface, which was simple. Tranquility. Whoever named you, by the way, performed a master stroke and perpetrated a huge joke on mankind."

"I'll tell Daddy you think so."

"I'll tell him myself. Along with a few other things." He cleared his throat. "You were tranquil, serene. Under that was your interest in people, and your understanding of them. Compassion. A willingness to help, whatever the cost to yourself. If you had it to give, you gave. If you didn't have what was needed, you found someone who did."

"Am I being canonized?"

"The worst is yet to come."

"I was afraid of that."

Brian kissed her, then cleared his throat again. "Under the compassion was something more complex. Your tendency to plot. It was as natural for you to take the devious way as it was for the Borgias to poison dinner guests."

Her expression was pensive as she said mildly, "I don't like the comparison."

"I call 'em as I see 'em."

Serena stared at him. "The next time I have you at my mercy, you're going to regret saying that."

"Consider me warned." He swallowed a laugh. "Where was I? Oh, yes. Your plotting. Entirely natural. And, coupled with the layer under it, your need to control, it makes for a truly frightening combination. With absolutely no malice, you very gently went about arranging things to suit you. People, as well as situations. The more tangled a situation became, the more you enjoyed it." He lifted a brow at her. "No comment?"

"I'm waiting to find out what my basic trait is," she said politely.

"Bear with me. Under the control, I decided on a layer of vulnerability. You are vulnerable, you know."

"I was beginning to wonder."

"I'm not surprised. But you do have that layer. However, under that is your basic trait. The trait that, in effect, influences every other trait. The strong, basic core of your personality."

"I'm afraid to ask." But she wasn't, because she knew that he understood her now.

Brian smiled very tenderly. "You can't bear to lose."

Serena returned his smile. "When I was six, Daddy explained about graciousness in the face of defeat. I didn't get it. I never have."

He laughed. "It was the only thing that made sense. And after that everything else fell into place. There was never one plot, there was a series of plots. All woven into a web I couldn't have escaped from no matter what I did." He sighed. "Once you'd made up your mind to catch me, *you never gave up.* Every step in every plan was based on that single determination. I nearly had it figured out this morning in the garden. I'd realized you were still plotting, but I hadn't realized what drove you."

"And I caught you," she murmured.

"You're a devious woman!" he told her sternly.

"Yes, but compassionate," she reminded him. "And I didn't force you to the altar, after all. I just created a situation that forced you to think about what you really wanted. The final decision was always yours, darling."

Brian stared at her for a moment, then said in

a very calm tone, "We're going to rewrite the vows, darling, because you're going to promise never to involve me in another of your plots without my prior knowledge and consent."

Serena smiled.

And, realizing what he'd just said, Brian smiled too. "No, you won't have to promise."

"You'll always know what I'm plotting," she agreed softly. "You'll be my best friend. No secrets. No tricks."

He surrounded her face in his warm hands. "I love you, Serena."

"And I love you." Her smile was tender, glowing. True to her nature, she immediately added, "Can we call room service? I'm starving."

A long time later, after room service had come and gone, and the ravages of Serena's day had been repaired, Brian watched his love take the phone off the hook.

"Why?" he asked curiously.

"Oh, because we don't want to be disturbed. Do we?"

Brian pulled her over on top of him. "No. But what makes you think we would be?"

"Call it a hunch."

"Why do I get the feeling one of your hunches might as well be considered an ironclad certainty?"

"I can't imagine."

Brian let it pass. "Tell me something." He smiled up at her. "That little scene in the garden this morning. If I *had* said it was over, if I'd walked away and said it was for good, what would you have done?"

"I would have . . ." Serena smiled very gently. "Thought of something."

He stared at her for a long moment, then began to laugh. "Oh, boy, what've I let myself in for?"

"Love." Serena laughed. "And me too. Because, darling, even when you didn't know you loved me, I've never felt so loved in my life."

Brian drew her head down, his green eyes darkening. "And I've never felt so tangled . . . in such a loving web."

When the operator reported the phone's being off the hook, Josh wasn't surprised. He thanked her and broke the connection. Then, after a moment's thought, he dialed a familiar number.

Stuart would already know, of course. He was psychic where Serena was concerned. He'd probably already chosen the wedding gift. Listening to the phone ring, Josh wondered idly about that blond pianist.

Could she be a brunette?

Solemnly he cursed Serena for her innocent comment.

THE EDITOR'S CORNER

Next month is an important landmark for all of us on the LOVESWEPT team—our fourth birthday! I received an absolutely wonderful letter a few months ago, and I decided to wait until now to share it with you, because its message is a real birthday tribute to LOVESWEPT. The letter came from a woman and her husband who have been married a long time. He is enthusiastic about televised sports; she is a romance reader who counts LOVESWEPT her favorite line. One Sunday afternoon while he was engrossed watching a game, his wife sat nearby reading a LOVESWEPT and chuckling and laughing aloud at various passages. Fortunately, her husband didn't get annoyed, only curious, and later that night he asked if he could borrow the book she had so obviously enjoyed. She loaned it to him. He loved it. He asked to read more of those "terrific stories." Their letter—a joint effort—thanked us not only for entertaining them so much, but also for helping to put a whole lot of new zing and zip into their relationship. I treasure this letter, as I treasure so many you've written to me through the years.

So what do we have for you on our birthday month? An especially merry—perhaps inspiring?—quartet of romances.

First, in talented Joan Elliott Pickart's **WILD POPPIES**, LOVESWEPT #190, you'll encounter a simply delightful couple. Heroine Courtney Marshall, a lovely young widow, decides she must go on a husband hunt to provide her two small children with a sweet, reliable father. Luke Hamilton is a gorgeous hunk of man who doesn't appear to be the least bit steady to Courtney so she immediately rules him out and tells him the reason! Luke is floored by Courtney's "quest" and more than a little worried about the fate of such a beautiful and innocent soul out there in the woods with all those big, bad wolves. (And Luke should

(continued)

know—he has howled with the best of them!) Protecting and pleasing Courtney are priorities for Luke that soon turn to fiery passion in this love story whose charms will linger with you for many a day.

Who would guess that behind the pretty face, just under the lovely blond hair of Iris Johansen lurks a whole universe of people, places, adventures, and love with all its joys and a few of its sorrows? A stranger wouldn't guess but all of us know, right? And next month Iris will tour you through places you've visited with her before and she'll reacquaint you with a few old friends while she delights you anew with a marvelous romance, **ACROSS THE RIVER OF YESTERDAY,** LOVESWEPT #191. Part cowboy, part cavalier, and all man, Gideon Brandt knew his footloose days were numbered the very second he saw violet-eyed Serena Spaulding. But Serena was bound to others by secrets and responsibilities that forced her to hide from Gideon for years. He'd searched the wide world for her . . . and when he recaptured her at last it was hardly the ideal place or time for a love to flourish. Yet, even as their very lives were threatened, their desire for each other blazed to white heat . . . a sensational love story!

Witty, whimsical, passionate are the words that readily describe **THE JOY BUS,** LOVESWEPT #192, by the very creative Peggy Webb. Ms. Jessie Wentworth, mistress of all she surveys and a workaholic of the first order, is alternately baffled and beguiled by devastatingly handsome Blake Montgomery. Blake is a professor using his sabbatical for meandering through the countryside and putting on the magic shows he finds such fun to do, all out of his pink touring bus! Wonderfully down to earth—and earthy!—Blake makes Jessie see stars—and even wish on them. But how could she be sure that their love for one another wasn't just another illusion? JOY BUS is—truly—a joy!

(continued)

The book Kay Harper has created for you for next month is so fast-paced, so full of surprises, so breath-taking in the passionate intensity of its romance, that the best place for you to read it would be in a plane because you'd have a seat belt and a ready supply of pure oxygen! Find the next best spot to settle in and fly away even without a plane with **RAVEN ON THE WING**, LOVESWEPT #193. The hero is a man you know very well from **IN SERENA'S WEB**, LOVESWEPT #189 this month. Joshua Long avoids brunettes as if they carried the plague, as you'll recall. He will only date blondes and Serena has clued us into the reason: Josh knows the woman of his dreams will be a brunette . . . and she'll put an end to his playboy days. His intuition was right. He meets his loving fate in the sexy shape of Raven Anderson, a woman as beautiful as she is enigmatic. When the maddeningly mysterious Raven disappears, Josh has to use all the formidable tools he can bring to hand . . . and in the process almost destroys the woman he only wants to cherish. This is a riveting love story!

I hope that in the year to come not one of our LOVESWEPTS will disappoint you.

Warm regards,

Carolyn Nichols

Carolyn Nichols
 Editor
LOVESWEPT
Bantam Books, Inc.
666 Fifth Avenue
New York, NY 10103